RELATIONSHIP MATERIAL

JENYA KEEFE

RIPTIDE
PUBLISHING

Riptide Publishing
PO Box 1537
Burnsville, NC 28714
www.riptidepublishing.com

Cover art: L.C. Chase, lcchase.com
Editors: Veronica Vega, Carole-ann Galloway
Layout: L.C. Chase, lcchase.com/design-portfolio.html

ISBN: 978-1-62649-902-7

First edition
August, 2019

Also available in ebook:
ISBN: 978-1-62649-879-2

RELATIONSHIP MATERIAL

JENYA KEEFE

RIPTIDE
PUBLISHING

For M, with love and hot coffee.

TABLE OF
CONTENTS

CHAPTER ONE

Evan Doyle practiced mindfulness.

He sat at an outdoor table in front of his favorite coffee shop, focusing on the sensations of the moment: the chill and dampness of the autumn air on his face and hands. The gold and red maple leaves that whirled through the air. The presence of his dog, curled at his feet under the table. The smell of his coffee in its warm ceramic mug, the inky smell of the folded newspaper it was holding down, open to the crossword puzzle. *Mother's sister, in Monterrey.* He clicked the top of his ballpoint pen and wrote *TIA.*

"Alex!" shouted a woman's voice.

He startled and felt Dulcie jump. That shout—that *name*—shattered Evan's calmness into a million shards. He looked up to see Caroline Farkas, standing there on the sidewalk across the street, staring at him.

He hadn't seen his sister in fifteen years.

Fear crawled all over his skin, raising his hair, tightening his guts, sucking the air out of his lungs. Caroline, one palm on her heart, opened her lips as if to shout *Alex* again. Evan made an instinctive, convulsive *shushing* gesture, and she put her hand over her mouth.

He stood up, almost knocking over his chair; said, "Come on," to Dulcie; and walked away, leaving his newspaper and coffee behind.

Evan turned right and hurried down a side street, his dog trotting at his heels. In the alley behind the coffee shop he waited. Even after all these years, he knew Caroline would follow: now that she'd seen him, she would never give up, so he might as well just wait. Dulcie stood alertly at his feet, waiting with him.

"Alex?"

His sister, very grown-up in a gray suit and white blouse, picked her way down the grubby alley toward him. She looked beautiful. Clean and professional, her sensible low heels tapping on the dirty asphalt. She didn't belong in an alley, with the coffee shop's dumpster, with the smell of damp and sour milk, with him.

No air seemed to be entering his lungs. He gulped for breath. His skin flushed, both hot and cold.

"Alex," she said, coming closer. She didn't know that each *Alex* was like a dart in his skin. Still unable to breathe, he braced himself on his knees, head hanging.

He was dying.

He knew what was happening, knew his fear was irrational: panic attacks weren't fatal and there was no danger from Caroline, of all people in the world. But his breath whistled in his throat, his heart hammered with terror. *Dying.*

Caroline was touching him. "Hey. It's okay. Alex, it's okay." Then Dulcie was there, pushing her away with a kind of wagging stubbornness. The dog shoved her cold nose against his hot face, ran back to Caroline, then back to him. Back to Caroline to shoulder her farther away, then back to Evan. He caught her in his arms and hugged her. She smelled of clean dog.

I'm dying. I'm dying. His skin and hands were prickling with paresthesia caused by hyperventilation. Dulcie had driven Caroline to the other side of the alley. Created a safe zone around Evan. He tried counting his breaths. Deep calming breaths from the diaphragm. It wasn't working. Dulcie leaned into Evan and he buried his face in her fur. *Breathe. Breathe.*

"Okay," Caroline was saying. "It's all right, Alex."

Eventually the diaphragm breathing and the press of Dulcie's body calmed him, as it always did. The irrational conviction of imminent death subsided. He managed to get his eyes open, uncurl from his crouch, wipe the sweat and tears off his face.

Caroline was leaning against the brick wall of the alley, arms held tightly across her chest, face white and taut.

"I'm okay," he whispered.

She nodded.

"I'm okay," he said again. *Just an anxiety attack. A little panic for no reason. I'm fine.* He was fine.

After a moment, he managed to say, "You'll mess up your clothes."

"I don't care about my clothes."

Once she'd agonized over her clothes. She used to comb the Goodwill aisles, alter her thrift-store finds with needle and thread so they'd fit better, so she could walk tall in their high school hallways. A proud teenage girl, driven to express herself and to fit in.

That had been fifteen years ago, of course. She wasn't that kid anymore. No doubt she was just as proud, just as resolute; but now she could probably afford to get that good suit cleaned.

"We can't talk here," he said.

"Okay," she agreed. "Where?"

"My place. Tomorrow." He looked up, met her eyes as fearlessly as he could. "Come alone, Caroline. Don't tell anyone you saw me. Don't let anyone follow you."

"Okay."

"I'm serious."

"I know." She pushed off the wall, took a step closer. Her hands opened and closed, and then she folded them tightly, as though she wanted to touch him and was holding herself back. "Tell me where."

He held out a hand, and she approached and took it. Her hand was cool and much smaller than his own. He gently turned it over, pushed up the sleeve of her blazer, fished his pen out of the pocket of his flannel shirt, and wrote his address on her arm, on the pale skin where the sleeve would cover it. "After lunch sometime. We'll talk. About everything."

She touched the messy blue ink on her skin with her free hand. "I'll be there," she said. "Will you?"

Would he? This was his chance. He had almost twenty-four hours to disappear. She must know he was thinking about it.

He met her eyes. "I'll be there."

"Alex?" she whispered. "Where have you been?"

"I'll tell you," he promised his twin. "Tomorrow."

"Goddamn it."

Evan stood at his kitchen window, looking out across his front yard, where a car was pulling off the main road and into his long gravel driveway. Two people were in the car, visible even from this distance.

Dulcie, out on the front porch, pointed her nose at the sky and gave her alarm bark—a high *woo-woo-woo*, immediately followed by hasty retreat through her dog door to his side in the kitchen, where she sat anxiously at his heels.

Dulcie was not much of a guard dog.

Evan was nervous too. He glanced around his place, wondering what Caroline would think of it. His house was an old A-frame cottage, out past the town of Corbett in the hills above the Columbia River Gorge. It used to be somebody's old fishing cabin, dilapidated, isolated, but with four acres of wooded land and its own icy rushing stream. Perfect for a paranoid recluse like himself. He'd bought it for a song, replaced the roof, stripped it to the studs, and was slowly renovating it, room by room. The kitchen and downstairs bathroom were done—new tiles, new countertops and fixtures, fresh paint. The rest of the house was plywood and dust, and the yard was a carpet of unraked fallen leaves.

The car made its slow way up the gravel driveway to the house and stopped behind Evan's pickup. Caroline got out from the driver's seat and stood for a moment, looking at the mountains, the stream, Evan's little house. She hadn't known how to drive when he'd seen her last. Neither of them had.

Slim and upright as a girl, his twin had grown up into a small woman, but she had a settled air about her now: confidence, instead of bravado. Her jaw was firm, and her gaze level. She wore jeans and a windbreaker, and her straight dark hair shone in the autumn sun.

A guy unfolded himself from the passenger side, and Evan clenched his hands on the countertop. He was tall, good-looking, and for God's sake he was wearing a charcoal suit and a red tie, in the Cascade Mountains, on a Saturday. He put his hands in his pockets, peering around, his expression one of refined distaste.

What a douche.

Dulcie, sensitive to his anxiety, made a crooning sound. "It's all right," he told her, hoping it was true.

Caroline and the douche were now coming up the walk toward the house. She seemed nervous, tucking her hair behind her ears. Their footsteps echoed hollowly on the boards of the porch. Dulcie woofed, and he said, "Go to bed." She went into the stripped living room and jumped up on the armchair there as Caroline knocked on the front door.

He let them in. Took Caroline's hand. It was cold.

"Hey," she said, a little hesitantly. "It's me."

"Hey, Kiki." He glanced at the tall guy in the suit and then back to Caroline. "You brought a friend."

"This is Malcolm Umbertini. Mal, Alex."

He didn't say anything. He just looked at her—and like always, she understood him as if he'd spoken aloud. He could tell, because she got right in his face, jabbed him in the chest with one finger, and said, "Shut up."

He glared.

Her eyes, clear blue and more familiar than his own, shone with furious tears. "*You* disappeared. Mom died. Derrick got killed right in front of my eyes. Where the hell were you? *Gone.* Gone. You have been gone for fifteen years and *I needed you*, Boxy. I needed you, and you weren't there, so you *don't* get to tell me that I can't go to someone else for help. Mal is my friend and he was there for me when you *weren't*. He's the person who is there for me when I need it, because you weren't around. And I needed help, so he's here, and that's *it*. Okay?"

"Okay," he managed to whisper. Her face went blurry; he was tearing up too. He pulled her into his arms.

She punched him in the shoulder, fairly hard, her lashes black with tears. "Okay?"

"Okay. I'm sorry. It's okay." He held her tight and pressed his face into her hair while she cried on his chest. "Shh, don't. I'm sorry."

Evan glowered over her shoulder at her friend. The one she had turned to since he hadn't been around.

The guy, Malcolm Umbertini, was seriously handsome, with olive skin and a long Italian nose, heavy-lidded brown eyes, full lips over a square jaw. His dark hair was neatly barbered and combed. He looked like Dean Martin's sexier brother.

He also looked like an asshole. He was standing with his hands on his hips, glancing around like he was afraid to get dust on his good clothes. His upper lip had a curl to it that resembled disdain.

"God," said Caroline, sniffling, stepping back from Evan and dashing tears out of her eyes. "I'm happy to see you, Boxy, but I'm so angry with you."

He nodded.

"Can I use your ba?"

He smiled, despite the tension. *Ba* was one of their many childhood words for everyday things, ones no one else used. "Through there."

"Okay." She retreated into the finished bathroom, leaving him with her tears on his shirt, alone with good old Mal.

He wiped his own eyes, turned away. "Have a seat," he said gruffly, gesturing to the card table with folding chairs where he ate his meals. "Want a cup of coffee? I mean, it's decaf."

"Sure."

"Cream or sugar or anything?"

"Black. She likes cream."

Of course fucking Malcolm Umbertini knew how Caroline took her coffee and Evan didn't. Neither of them had drunk coffee fifteen years ago.

He pulled a little carton of cream out of the refrigerator and set it on the table, then reached up into the cabinet for cups. He poured the coffee and then turned, just in time to catch Mal checking out his ass.

He blinked at him; Mal lifted his eyes to meet Evan's without shame or hesitation. Instant, unmistakable recognition.

Evan held Mal's gaze as he set a brimming coffee cup down in front of him. "So," he drawled, "how long have you been dating my sister?"

Mal smiled, a slightly one-sided curl of his lips that revealed a vertical dimple and a slice of sharp white teeth. A snarl of a smile. Maybe even a sneer of a smile.

"Fair question," he said. "We're friends. She knows I'm gay." Mal had a big voice, a kind of rich flexible baritone, every word clearly enunciated like he was performing on a stage. He sipped the coffee in a leisurely fashion, his eyebrows going up a little in challenge. "Does she know *you're* gay?"

"Unless she thinks I've changed," retorted Evan. This guy was unbelievable. "Hey, Kiki," he called, as Caroline emerged from the bathroom. "Did you know I'm gay?"

Caroline looked flushed and damp, but composed. "Why, have you changed?" she asked. "You told me you wanted to marry Brian Littrell when you were eleven."

"Backstreet Boy," said Mal surprisingly. "Solid choice."

Caroline took off her jacket and sat down at the card table. "Wonder what Brian Littrell's been doing for the last fifteen years?"

"Being straight, I'm pretty sure," Evan said, putting Mal out of his mind. "Want some do? No caffeine."

"Sure."

He filled cups, set them on the table, fetched some spoons for the cream. "If I recall, you preferred Justin Timberlake." He sat beside her.

"Yes, well. My taste in boys has always been kind of a problem," she admitted.

"Yeah?"

"Yeah. Were you dating Manuel Hernandez in high school?"

He smiled at the memory. He hadn't thought of Manny Hernandez in years. "Oh, yeah, but 'dating' might not be the right word."

Caroline's eyes flicked down to the carton—heavy whipping cream, full fat—and there was cool assessment in her gaze. She didn't take any.

There was so much to say. So many explanations, excuses, apologies. He didn't even know how to start. The pressure of all the things he needed to say, but didn't know how, sat like lead in his chest.

His very first therapist, the one his foster parents had taken him to when he'd been deep in the awful throes of recovery, had talked to him about balance. She'd said it was natural to avoid the things that frightened you, but you couldn't avoid the people who love you. *"Don't reject people because you're afraid they'll reject you,"* she'd said. *"You have to try to find a balance."*

Just start.

"First off, you need to know this." He pulled his wallet from his pocket and gave her his driver's license. "Accounts of the death of Alex Farkas are completely true. This is my legal identity now."

"Evan Doyle," said Caroline, fingering the plastic rectangle. "Irish name."

"We could be Irish," he said.

She smiled. "We could. Hey, you're older than me now."

She'd been born six hours before him. "Sorry about that."

"WITSEC?" asked Mal.

Evan glanced Mal's direction. He had been successfully ignoring him. "The state version. CalWRAP. California Witness Relocation and Assistance Program." He sipped his decaf. "You can't call me Alex anymore. It's dangerous, not just for me. You nearly gave me a heart attack yesterday, Caroline."

"I noticed. Witness protection?"

Her voice and expression were neutral. Was she skeptical? No. He'd talked to a lot of lawyers in his day, and they all did this. It was an open-ended question, clearly designed to elicit an explanation. "It's a long story," he said. "The danger seemed real at the time. It still does."

"What are you doing in Portland?"

"I got a job here two years ago. I thought you were in Baltimore."

"I was. Four years ago I moved here." She extended the license between her fingers. "So you didn't come here to find me."

"No. I'm sorry. I didn't know. I wouldn't have dared come if I did." He took the ID, put his wallet back into his pocket. "I'm sorry I stayed away. I'd have come sooner, if I thought it was safe."

She bit the inside of her cheek. "Can I still call you Boxy?"

"I think so. Yeah, Kiki."

He wanted to hold her hands, to hug her again, but she was sitting rigidly, gripping her cup in front of her. In spite of her calm appearance, the cup trembled.

Unexpectedly, she smiled. "So you finally got a gie."

Relieved, he smiled back at her. "Yeah." How they'd longed for a gie of their own, when they were kids. "Her name is Dulcie."

Hearing her name, Dulcie hopped down from her chair and came into the room, toenails tapping on the floor. Caroline unbent and patted her thigh, and Dulcie approached her, tail wagging, to have her head stroked.

"Is she a therapy animal?"

"Yes, and she cost an arm and a leg." Then he answered the question behind her question. One of them. "I have chronic anxiety. She's great."

"I saw how she was with you." She ruffled the soft fur behind Dulcie's ears. "Do you have someone now? Boyfriend?"

"Not so much," he admitted. "You? Do you have a family?"

"My job," she said, lifting one thin shoulder slightly.

"I never thought you'd be a lawyer," he said. "I thought you wanted to be a math teacher."

"Well, that day changed everything," she said, and they both knew what day she meant: the day their mother had died, the day he'd left home. "I wanted to help victims of crimes."

He noticed that he was fiddling with a spoon, and put it down. "So, just the job?"

"Some good friends. I do have a boyfriend, but he's probably not long-term."

That was sad. She deserved to be loved by someone steady. How hard had the years been for her, alone? Her wrists were thin, and there were blue smudges under her eyes. She hadn't taken any cream in her coffee, even though her friend Mal had said she liked it. "Are you still playing the Food Game, Caroline?"

Caroline's soft blue eyes saw right into the middle of his heart, just like always. "Two thousand calories a day, whether I want 'em or not. Are you?"

He smiled at her and poured about a hundred calories into his coffee, then set the carton down firmly in front of her. She pressed her lips together and added some cream to her cup too.

CHAPTER TWO

I f Mal wasn't mistaken, Alex Farkas had just goaded Caro into adding cream to her coffee.

Mal wished he could vanish into the woodwork as Caro and her brother stared each other down over decaf, their profiles near mirror-images of each other. He knew that Caro struggled with an eating disorder; he was mildly impressed that her brother seemed to know that as well, given that he hadn't seen her in— How long had she said? Fifteen years? Mal had assumed the eating disorder had started *after* her mother died, but if Evan knew, it was older than that.

"I didn't even expect you to be here this afternoon," Caro was saying. "I thought we'd get here and find out you'd given me a fake address. Given me the slip. Are you going to disappear again?"

"I—" started Alex. *Evan*, Mal reminded himself. "I maybe should. I—I really like my job, though. And I own this place. Me and the bank, I mean. I don't want to keep running. I like it here."

Mal certainly hoped Evan wasn't planning to split. Caro would be shattered, and he would be the one to pick up the pieces. Caro Farkas was one of the few people who had never let Mal down, not once. She was the sister he'd never had, the family he'd chosen. He'd do anything for her. Even sit at this table where he was not wanted, drinking decaf that he did not like, and listening to a conversation that was none of his business.

And Caro needed the support. Her mother had been murdered and her brother had vanished when she was sixteen. It was a calamity from which she'd never entirely recovered. The loss of Alex, especially, had left a gaping wound that no one could ever fill. She had a tiny tattoo of an *x* over her heart—the missing variable, the lost piece of her life.

Now here he was, Caro's brother, gone so long he was almost a myth.

Mal shifted in his chair, hoping his discomfort wasn't obvious. That morning, he had tried to refuse to come along on this visit, but Caro had begged him.

"Listen, odds are good that he won't even be there. And if he is there, he might not want to talk to me. He might feed me some bullshit story."

"Why do you think that?"

"I don't know who he is anymore, but I do know he's a survivor of trauma. You should have seen him. Even if he wants to tell me everything—which is a big if—it'll be tough for him to face." Mal's reluctance must have shown in his expression, because she'd added, "Mal, you're good at this. I need you to help keep the conversation moving forward. Ask the hard questions."

"You're just as good."

"You think so?" She'd pursed her lips. "Maybe normally. But I survived some of the same stuff. Come on, Mal. Ask the questions that are too hard for me. Help me cut through the bullshit—including mine."

Now she asked Evan, "Where did you go? That Thanksgiving when we were sixteen?"

"You know where I was that day," said Evan.

"I don't," she said. "I was at the kitchen table doing my calculus homework. Mom and Derrick were in the En. You'd started vanishing that summer. I never knew where you went."

"I was in the En."

Caro's eyebrows drew together.

"Keep the conversation moving." Mal asked, "What's the En?"

When Caro didn't answer, Evan glanced at Mal and explained, "Our house had a detached garage with a little studio apartment upstairs. Mom said that we were going to rent it out for more income."

"We called it the Eagle's Nest for a joke," said Caro. "Later we shortened it to E.N., and then just En."

"We never did rent it out, because then she met her boyfriend, Derrick," said Evan. "By the time we were in high school, she was spending most of her time up there partying with him and his friends."

It wasn't quite the bullshit Mal had been warned about, but *boyfriend*, *partying*, and *friends* were euphemisms. Derrick Lee Sanders had been Kimberly Farkas's dealer and pimp. Caro knew that, but Evan didn't know that Mal knew it too.

"And that summer," Evan said slowly, "I started partying with them."

She nearly dropped her cup. "You did what?"

"I know I didn't tell you," said Evan, reaching across the table for her hands, "but I always thought you knew."

"*You were a child*," Caro cried. Her face went red, her eyes filling with tears again. Instead of taking his hands, she crossed her arms tightly, tucking her fists into her armpits.

Mal was similarly horrified. He felt a stab of compassion for the boy Evan had been. A minor, dragged into a world of hard drugs and prostitution? It would have been a desperately bad situation.

"Hey, don't cry." Evan kept his hands outstretched on the table.

"Did she know?" demanded Caro, her voice hoarse. "Did she know?"

"Yeah. She knew. She was there."

"How could she let you? How could she?"

"Kiki, please," he begged softly.

Sniffling, she unfolded herself, rested her hands in her brother's. He clasped them, and his eyes were wet now too. "Please, you gotta keep it together. This isn't even the bad stuff."

"It gets *worse*?"

"Yeah," said Evan again, laughing a little. "This is the happy part of the story."

"Oh, Alex, *why*?"

"Evan," he corrected her. "It seemed like a good idea at the time."

There was the bullshit. Mal and Caro both stared at her brother incredulously. He looked just as upset, his eyes red-rimmed, but he only squeezed her hands.

Mal judged, from the stubborn set of Evan's jaw, that it wouldn't be productive to press this point. *Why* was often a dead-end line of questioning anyway; better to nail down the sequence of events before delving into the reasons behind them.

There was a box of tissue on the kitchen counter, and Mal got up and brought it back to the table. Both siblings wiped their eyes.

Evan's dog sat up at his feet with a drama-queen sigh, and pointedly pawed at his thigh.

Mal said, "Is she distracting you on purpose?"

"Yep." Evan petted the dog. "She can tell I'm getting keyed up in here."

Caro followed Mal's lead, changing the subject for a lighter one. "Manny Hernandez got Arista Jones pregnant senior year. I went to their wedding."

"Really? Well, junior year he liked dick. Maybe it was just a phase."

Caro laughed weakly through her tears. Mal sipped his coffee patiently, as she blew her nose and visibly gathered her strength. She was, despite her pretty looks, one of the toughest people he knew. When he thought she was ready, he prompted, "Thanksgiving Day."

Caro looked at Mal gratefully, and turned back to Evan. "Yes. Let's do this. Thanksgiving Day. I was doing my calculus homework at the kitchen table. You were—"

"In the En," said Evan. "With Mom and Derrick. And the guy Derrick had brought over that day. His name was John Nesbit Everett. His buddies called him Nez." He took a deep, steadying breath. "He'd just gotten out of prison after a two-year term for stalking and assault."

Oh shit.

"And . . . and things got kind of out of hand."

Mal raised his eyebrows but said nothing. If he were interviewing Evan, he'd allow this evasion and circle back to it later.

But Caro couldn't do that, not today. "Is that who killed them?" she demanded. "John Nesbit Everett killed Mom and Derrick?"

Evan said nothing, his face white, his eyes down.

"You must have witnessed it," she pressed. "I saw Derrick come flying out the window. I saw him hit the pavement. The police said that the third man in the En must have killed them both. They never found him. Or you."

"I . . . Yes. I saw it all."

Caro gulped for breath. "Sorry," she said. "Just a second." With dignity, she stood up and walked out of the kitchen. The bathroom door shut behind her with a bang, and then the sound of her throwing up clearly reached them in the kitchen.

"I guess I need to soundproof that bathroom better," sighed Evan.

While Caro took her break, Evan sent Dulcie back to her chair and got up, unasked, and filled Mal's coffee cup.

So this was awkward. Here Mal was in Evan's kitchen, drinking his decaf, having just engaged in a deep-dive into his most awful memories. Evan's stony expression suggested he didn't enjoy this particular intimacy. The fact that Caro wanted him here must be the only reason Evan was tolerating his presence.

Mal had the fidgety urge to put him at ease, somehow; to assure him of his friendly intentions. *I'm not here to judge you*, he wanted to say.

"This house is beautiful," he tried instead. "Or will be, I think, when it's done."

"Thanks."

"Do you have a contractor? Or are you doing the work yourself?"

"Myself, bit by bit." Evan wasn't looking at him. "How did you meet Caroline?"

"First day of law school," said Mal. "One-L orientation, University of Virginia. We had a lot in common—we both paid for school by cobbling together loans and scholarships and things. Then we had classes together, because we both wanted to be criminal prosecutors." Mal could leave out details too: he and Caro had both been haunted by their pasts, and with no family to turn to they'd become family to each other. "After graduation we stayed in touch," he continued. "I got a job out here working for the Multnomah County DA. She went to work for Baltimore County, which is a much tougher gig than Multnomah. I missed her, and I knew she was getting burned out, so when a position opened up here, I suggested she apply for it."

While he spoke, he surreptitiously studied Evan. He and Caro had the same jaw and nose. They both had pale skin and high cheekbones and wide curving mouths too. Caro's eyes were a clear blue, though, while Evan's were darker: blue-gray, storm clouds to her sunny sky. His hair was fairer and shaggier than Caro's sleek brown locks. And of course to Mal—because he was wired that way—Evan was much more attractive. His body looked lean and hard in his scruffy jeans and rumpled T-shirt. Mal kept picturing him doing manual labor on the house. With, perhaps, wrenches and hammers and power tools and things.

Hot.

Way, way off-limits.

"She didn't want to be a lawyer back then, but she was always good at talking," said Evan, abruptly. "She learned to talk before I did. When we were kids, she was always the one who spoke for us." He fiddled with his coffee cup. "Is she a good lawyer?"

"Oh yes," said Mal, without hesitation. "She's one of the best. Meticulous, organized, thorough. Driven to seek justice. Which is what we're supposed to be, but not all of us are."

"That sounds like her."

Mal sipped his coffee. "So what do you do?"

"I'm a nurse."

That was unexpected. Mal blinked, and one corner of Evan's mouth twisted a little. "An RN? Or an LPN?"

"An RN."

"With chronic anxiety?" Most of Mal's encounters with nurses were ER staff, giving evidence of crimes: they seemed unflappable.

"Yeah."

"It isn't too stressful?"

Evan glared at him. "No," he said coolly. "You're kind of a prick, you know that?"

Mal sighed. So much for building rapport.

"Caro and I could give the exact same close," he said. "The jury will be persuaded by her, while they'll think I'm an arrogant motherfucker and acquit to spite me." Evan squinted at him, and Mal smiled. "I've got a jerk face. Can't help it. What I said about nursing wasn't a dig, you know. Just a question."

"Huh," said Evan skeptically. "So your jerk face is, what, a liability?"

"Oh, occasionally it comes in handy."

Evan's lips tightened. Nope, no rapport here—Evan plainly did not like him. Now he was avoiding Mal's eyes, looking toward the bathroom, where splashing water could be heard.

Mal liked Evan, though. It wasn't just that he was damn good-looking. Or that Mal was currently between boyfriends and bored with the dating scene. Evan had a lucent emotional transparency, even in his reluctance to discuss his past, that drew Mal's interest. He seemed to communicate his feelings instantly, with eyes and mouth and shoulders. Evan Doyle could *not* play poker.

Evan's man would always know exactly where he stood.

Caro finally reemerged, damp and puffy-eyed but composed. "I'm sorry I keep running off. This is kind of hard."

"I know," said Evan. "For me too. Are you okay?"

"Dandy." She smiled weakly and sat back down. "All right. Have we gotten to the bad part of the story yet?"

The dog, Dulcie, answered that question by immediately hopping down from her chair and rejoining the group. Evan scratched the dog's nape, and Mal found himself staring at Evan's big hands, gentle on the dog's velvet ears.

Stop that.

Caro said briskly, "All right. Mom died of a blow to the side of the head that fractured her skull and drove bone fragments into her brain. Medical examiners said she would have died almost instantly. Was that true?" Evan, white-faced, said nothing, and Caro persisted, "Alex? Tell me what happened."

"*Evan.*" His voice was husky; he looked like he was going to throw up next. "Call me Evan. Yes. It was fast. And she— Can we—can we . . . not? Right now?"

Caro's mouth hardened. Mal thought she would persist, so he rapped his knuckles lightly on the table. "Why don't we move on, and come back to that later?"

Evan glanced at Mal with what might almost be gratitude, and Caro blew out a breath. "Okay," she said. "We can leave that for now. Can you tell us what happened next? Where did you go, after?"

Evan said softly, "Well. So then, after what happened in the En. Um. I ended up . . . in a house in El Centro. I stayed there for a while. And the people there were sort of mid-level in an organization that imported meth from Mexico, and this house in El Centro, where I—where I stayed, was like a distribution point for meth."

No explanation of why he'd gone there, why he hadn't come back, or what had happened in between the En and El Centro. Caro's eyes met Mal's for an infinitesimal moment. This time they both let it slide.

"The people who lived there would cut the meth and repackage it and send it on to dealers in different cities," Evan went on. "They were also using, so I guess they weren't very careful. The place was raided by the cops thirteen days after I got there, and we were all—um, me included—arrested."

Caro asked curiously, "What was the charge against you?"

"Possession with intent to sell."

"A felony," said Mal. "Were you guilty?"

Evan glared at him. "No."

"What happened next?" asked Caro.

"I talked," said Evan. "What I shoulda done months earlier. I talked and talked and talked. Lawyers and cops and more lawyers. I gave them the names of all the people who'd been in and out of that house, and their relationships to each other, and everyone they'd ever mentioned. I have a good memory," he added, in an aside to Mal. "And I understood Spanish pretty well. People said things in front of me all the time. I knew where the drugs came from and where they were going, and how the dealers laundered the money, and who they paid and when and how. I knew all kinds of stuff that the cops could use, and the lawyers. And I told them *everything*."

"That was really brave, Boxy," said Caro softly.

"I don't know about that," said Evan. "Brave. No. I was just . . . stripped down to nothing at that point. Nothing mattered. But . . . so, CalWRAP kept me safe in a hotel for a few months, and then there were a lot of arrests, including Pablo Icaza, who was a fairly powerful organized-crime guy."

"It go to trial?" asked Mal.

"No, none of them. They all, what, settled? Pled guilty to one thing or another."

"That's good," said Caro. "Because most of what you heard wouldn't have been admissible at trial."

"I guess what I told the cops led them to more evidence," said Evan. "I don't know. I know that people went to prison. And I got a new name." He paused. "I wanted to call you, Caroline. So bad. They said you'd be in danger. They told me the cartel would come after you to flush me out."

"I got your postcard."

"Did you? Wasn't supposed to send that. Wasn't sure if I should, but I couldn't bear for you to think— Well." He smiled a little. "So that's how I ended up. What about you? Was it bad?"

"It was pretty bad." Caro's voice was crisp. "I lived with Jerry and June Willows until I graduated from high school."

"Ugh," said Evan.

Caro smiled a hard smile. "Yes, we went to church a lot, and they enjoyed having me around to pity. Then I got a full ride to UCLA."

"Awesome, you."

"Merit plus need. And then I went to Virginia for law school, which was as far away from Barstow as I could get. And now here I am. What about you?"

"I got my GED, and community college, and lots of therapy."

"Oh, me too," said Caro. "*Lots* of therapy."

They toasted each other with their coffee cups, smiling identical wry smiles.

Half an hour or so later, as Mal and Caro walked through fallen leaves toward the car, he demanded the keys for the drive back to Portland.

"I'm okay to drive," said Caro.

"You are wrung out like a dishrag. Give."

So he drove down the winding road through green-and-gold autumn forests, and she curled up in the passenger seat, hugging herself.

"What do you think?" he asked her, after a few miles. Evan had clammed up once he'd told them about El Centro. After that, he'd kept turning the conversation back to Caro, away from himself.

Both twins had seemed exhausted, so Mal had invented another engagement and ended the reunion.

"I don't know," she said, bumping her forehead against her drawn-up knees. "I'm so happy to see him, but . . ."

"It's a lot to process," agreed Mal. "Why do you call him Boxy?"

"Oh, that's old. Old story." He waited. Eventually she said, "We had this alphabet book. Each page was a different letter—'A is for Apple,' and so on. *X* was for 'box.' It was the only page where the letter was at the end of the word. Like Alex, right? So I started calling him Box." She glanced over at him. "I didn't say it was a good story."

"And Kiki?"

"That's even older. He couldn't pronounce Caroline at first, so he called me Ca. Caca. Then someone told us what that meant. So it was Coco, or Cuckoo. Kiki stuck, eventually. No one called me Caro until college."

"'Do' is coffee?"

"I think it was originally juice. We didn't drink coffee." She shifted, putting her feet up on the dashboard, hugging her knees. "*Why*? He never said why. We had plans. We were going to go to college and get out of that town. Why did he start to go to the En at all?"

"Drugs?"

"I wouldn't have thought so. And then why did he leave? Why did he go to that house?"

"He was a kid. He just ran."

"He would have come to me, if he could," she said. "We were so close."

Mal wasn't so sure. Teenagers pushed for independence and privacy; they pushed away from the familiar and the safe. By the time their mother died, young Alex had already started living his life without consulting Caro—the drugs, the boy he'd been hooking up with.

"Tell you what," she said, sitting up straight. "You research the meth house, and I'll research the guy. What was his name?"

"John Everett Nesbit. Or John Nesbit Everett. One of those. Alias Nez. But, Caro, Evan might not like us digging into this."

"Mal, he told us no more than twenty percent of the story."

"I know, but—"

"That guy killed my mother," she said flatly. "Why have I never heard his name before? That case is still open. Why? I have been all over every page of every file, and this Nez was never followed up as a lead. Why? Where is he now?"

"I'm not saying you should let this drop."

"I can't."

"I know. Of course not. I just think you should wait for Evan to talk to you. I don't think he'll like us turning over all his old history."

She sighed. "He might not," she admitted. "It must have been bad."

"Yep."

"He seemed okay, though. Sort of. Didn't he?"

"Yeah," said Mal. "He told me he's an RN. That means a college degree." They both knew, too well, that outcomes for teen runaways and sex workers were usually ugly. If half of what he suspected about Evan were true, then his house, college degree, and full-time profession were a triumph. "Not too bad, all things considered."

"And nursing is a stressful job," said Caro.

Mal grinned. "He called me a prick for mentioning that."

She snorted. "Well, he's not afraid to stand up for himself."

"That is the fucking truth." Evan Doyle seemed like a fighter. Battered and scarred, maybe, but still a fighter.

"He knows me," she said, after a pause. "He knows that I'm not going to be able to let this go."

Mal nodded. "I'm sure he'll tell you more when he comes over on Friday. Do you want me to join you?"

"No, leave me alone with him for the afternoon. We'll see if he opens up to me more when you're not there. Bring takeout in the evening."

"Okay." The road that took them back toward the interstate was narrow and winding, and Mal kept his eyes on it as he said, "So. I happened to notice that he's got a truly fantastic ass."

"Seriously, Mal, we're talking about my brother here."

"I know," he said. "I'm sorry. But I liked him, and he's really easy on the eyes."

"You're kidding me with this."

"I'm asking permission, Caro," he said tentatively.

"No."

Oh.

Caro was one of the two most important people in Mal's life. He'd never do anything to jeopardize their friendship. He wouldn't even risk the possibility. So if she wanted him to keep his hands off her brother, well, then his hands were off. "Okay."

But he was disappointed. And also a little hurt.

"No," she said again. "That's not what I mean. But, Mal—did you listen to the story he just told us?"

Mal navigated a hairpin turn, eyes on the road. "Yes?"

"Don't you think he seems kind of messed up?" she said. "All raw nerves and jitters. He didn't use to be so jagged."

"He's got guts."

"He's got *issues*. You get so serious so fast, and you've got a thing for wounded guys."

"That's a low blow, Caro." He frowned at her. "This isn't like that."

"You don't know if it's like that or not."

"Well, there's one obvious difference."

"I'm just saying. You don't have to collect one of each possible dysfunction. You deserve someone stable."

He took a moment to dart a glare at her. "You don't exactly have a lot of high ground, sweetheart. Unless you've forgotten about the two married guys *in a row* who—"

"I know!" she said, throwing up her hands. "I know. My taste in men is terrible. I'm not denying it."

"You couldn't if you tried."

"You like Paul."

He did not actually particularly care for Paul, Caro's current boyfriend, but he declined to be distracted by this comment. "I like Evan," he said. "But if you want me to drop it, I will." She didn't say anything, so he added, "Ah, it's probably wishful thinking, anyway. When you were telling him all about how I had replaced him as your brother, I thought he was going to leap over the table and punch me in the mouth."

She leaned her head on his shoulder. "You did, you know."

He smiled. "Leave it to a little sister to sabotage my prospects with hot boys."

"I'll put in a good word for you on Friday."

"You don't have to do that."

"I'll only tell him the truth."

"Nooo," he cried. "Curse your sudden yet inevitable betrayal."

"Malcolm." She ruffled his hair, and, annoyed, he smoothed it back down again. "I think you are the best thing that could happen to any guy, including my brother. But he might not be the best thing that could happen to you."

CHAPTER THREE

"**A**re you still in touch with your foster family?" asked Caroline, offering Evan a glass of iced tea.

It was Friday evening, and Evan was ensconced on Caroline's couch in her tiny bungalow, a few blocks off Hawthorne in east Portland.

"Tricia and Gordon," he said, accepting the glass. "Not really, just Christmas cards and things like that. They didn't try to be, like, parents."

Friday was the first day of his weekend, and she'd taken the day off so they could have uninterrupted time to get to know each other again. He'd arrived at noon, and they'd been talking for hours now. Evan hadn't talked this much in years. While Dulcie slept peacefully, they'd compared notes on careers (both satisfactory), relationships (Caroline's mostly disastrous, Evan's mostly nonexistent), and all the other details of their lives.

"Lucky you," Caroline said, sitting at the other end of the couch. On the TV in the corner, a low-volume Marvel Cinematic Universe marathon was playing, unwatched. "That's one of the things that annoyed me about the Willowses. They were all, 'We're your new family now.' I think they expected me to be so grateful that I'd forget I already had a family."

Caroline had clearly not forgotten. The iced tea was sweetened exactly the way their mother had made it. When she'd proudly given him a tour of her house earlier—striped pink-and-white wallpaper, eyelet curtains and antique furniture—he'd been struck by how similar the style was to that of their childhood home. Mom would have loved it. Evan wondered if that was deliberate, or if maybe Caroline was unconscious of how similar her taste was to their mother's.

Shaking off old memories, he asked, "Did the Food Game ever get bad for you?"

"Yes, it did."

"Me too," he said. "Seemed like such a harmless habit when we were kids, didn't it? But yeah, later, it got bad."

The Food Game hadn't just seemed harmless: it had seemed positive, the smart thing to do. Their mother would, when she remembered, stock the kitchen with expired food stolen from the grocery store where she'd worked. Then each evening she'd retire to the En, leaving them to feed themselves. They'd preferred canned and frozen food to fresh, both because it was less likely to be spoiled, and because they'd liked to keep track of the nutritional information on the labels. They'd felt so adult and wise, taking care of themselves and each other.

"It landed me in the hospital," she said. "I had an affair with a married professor when I was in college, and after that I don't think I ate for a month."

"Jesus, Kiki," said Evan. "At UCLA, or UV?"

"UCLA."

"Should I go break his neck?"

"Nah. He's lost his tenure now. I guess he made a habit of it, grazing among the undergrads. Some of the girls—not me, obviously—made a stink about it. I just took to my bed like a tragic flower, until my roommate figured out what I was doing and called an ambulance."

"Fuck. It was that bad?"

"About ninety-five pounds at my worst. You?"

"Not . . . No. Not that bad. I was in protective custody with CalWRAP, and then with Tricia and Gordon until I turned eighteen. They couldn't help but notice that I was having panic attacks every five seconds and refusing to eat anything that didn't come in a box. They figured it out right away. Taught me to cook fresh food. Got me pills and meal plans and therapy."

"It took me longer." She smiled suddenly. "Learning to cook food that didn't come from cans and boxes is one of the hardest things I've ever done."

"Oh, me too. I remember trying to explain to Tricia that boxes were better because they're labeled."

"Right? The lack of USDA nutritional information printed on fresh vegetables has annoyed me for years."

They laughed together. It was amazing to be able to laugh about this. It was amazing to be with Caroline again, and to find that they still understood each other so well. He'd talked to lots of other people who had complicated relationships with food, but no one else in the world would ever understand the appalling rituals of *their* Food Game. And definitely no one else would laugh about them with him.

Caro curled her legs up under her on the flowered couch, looked down into her iced tea glass. After a long moment, she said, "I know it's hard to talk about, but I have to know. Why did you do it? Why did you start going up to the En?"

He breathed, slowly. Mindfulness: the cold smoothness of the glass in his hands, the smell of the tea, the faint sound of the heater, blowing warm air into the room. "Derrick," he said finally. "I used to . . . I used to climb up on the roof of the garage and listen to what was happening in there. Did you ever do that?"

"Uh, no," she said. "Gross."

"I was curious," he said defensively.

"I was in denial. Go on."

"So one time I heard a guy in the En, asking about you. 'The little one in the house.' Derrick said you weren't available. But you . . . you know. It was the summer we turned sixteen. It seemed like Derrick was looking at you a lot." He paused. "He was looking at you like . . . not like he wanted you himself, but like something he could use. You were pretty and young, and he was looking at you like a pimp."

Caroline's brow wrinkled.

"I thought," said Evan carefully, "and I know it was really stupid, Kiki, but I thought it was my job to protect you. So I went to Derrick and told him I'd do it. We made a deal. He'd leave you alone, and I'd go to the En."

Caroline drew in a breath. She'd gone pale.

"I wasn't a virgin," he went on. "I mean, just barely. I'd been giving blowjobs to Manny, and I thought I could handle it. A couple blowjobs a week to guys. I thought that would be no big deal. I thought I could control the situation better than you could have. Because I was the man, I guess, is what I thought."

"No. Oh, Box."

"Yeah," he said. "I didn't touch the drugs. But I did what the men wanted. I even got paid." He smiled at her. "It wasn't so bad."

Caroline's brow crinkled, her mouth stretched. She was crying again. "You did it because of me? To protect *me*?"

He put down his glass, dragged her into his arms. He held her hard and said into her hair, "Listen. It wasn't your fault. It was not your fault. It was—it was the dumbest, stupidest, most arrogant decision I ever made in my life. Everything bad that happened afterward came from that one stupid choice. I was a dumb kid who thought he was the man of the family, and it was not—*not* your fault."

"It was hers," she said, raging through her tears. "It wasn't your job to protect me. It was hers, her job to protect us both."

He cuddled her tighter. His lungs ached with tension and he drew a deliberate breath, trying to relax his diaphragm. He wished their reunion could be nothing but happy memories, but that was never going to be true, not since the first moment she'd yelled his name on the street.

"I should have talked to someone," he said, his voice a whisper. "I don't know why I didn't. I've thought about it a million times. Why didn't I get help? I could have gone to a teacher, or the cops, or—or even Manny Hernandez. I don't know. I just . . . Someone would have stopped it, if I hadn't kept it a secret. But I did. It honestly never occurred to me to get help. I was so dumb."

"Because that's what we did," she said, wiping her eyes. "We kept her secret. God, do you think I don't remember how it was? We spent all our time being perfect, so that no one would come over or look too close, so that no one would ever find out about Mom. That was just how it had always been."

"I'm sorry," he said again, inadequately. "I wish I had been smarter."

"You don't have to be sorry." Her face was grave, her eyebrows crooked. "It's not true that everything bad came from your decision. There were lots of bad decisions, made by all of us." She pressed her lips together. "I'll never forgive her," she vowed, sniffling. "I've been fighting with myself about her for so long. I've told myself that she was poor and alone. But no matter what, I'll never forgive her for not protecting you."

She was still so angry, so full of fire. When he thought of their mother, it was with a sort of tired pity. "I think I have."

She gazed at him through her tears. "Ugh. You're so *well-adjusted*."

"Oh yeah, that's me," he agreed, and, surprising him, she began to laugh.

After a moment she got up, still chuckling, to wash her face. She came back with refills of the iced tea. "I'm booking another therapy session this week." Her voice was still rusty with tears, but her chin was high, her smile bright, if a little hard. "Thank God for government benefits. They cover mental health care. Do you still go to therapy?"

He accepted the change of subject as well as the tea. "Yeah. I'm not a regular anymore, but I still go sometimes. Or I'll go to an anxiety group."

"Are you kidding? It was all I could do to not bite people in group."

"Group makes me feel like I'm helping people. Gets me out of my own head."

"Uh-huh," said Caroline. "You're *that* person. The one who encourages everyone else to share, and tells them how great they're doing."

"Yeah. And you're the one who's all, 'Eat shit, you losers.'"

They grinned at each other in mutual recognition, and Evan added, "The other thing about support groups is that they're a really bad place to pick up dates."

"Obviously?" She raised her eyebrows.

"Seems obvious now, doesn't it?" She had told him about her college professor; he wanted to tell her this. "I dated a girl from group when I was, oh, eighteen. We knew way too much about each other's needs and vulnerabilities and buttons and levers."

"Sounds like a recipe for codependency."

"It was. And it went on too long. We didn't treat each other well, but we didn't know how to get out of it. I'm not very proud of how it went down."

Caroline sipped her tea. Behind her, the end credits of *Iron Man 2* scrolled, unnoticed. "Mal Umbertini thinks you're hot."

"Get the fuck out of here."

She laughed. "He likes you."

"Nope." Evan picked up the remote and clicked to start the next movie in the queue: *Thor*.

"Why are you rejecting the idea without even thinking about it?" asked Caroline.

"Because *no*. Why would you try to set me up with Mal Umbertini?"

"I'm not. But he does like you. And he's a good guy, you know, Boxy."

He leaned forward on the couch and ruffled her hair. "I'm glad you like him, Kiki. I'm glad he was there for you after everything got so fucked up." He pulled away to meet her eyes. "But if you think a guy like that is going to get with me, you're crazy."

"What do you mean by 'a guy like that'?"

"I mean he's a dick."

"He's— Okay, no, he's not *nice*," she said. "I know he looks all cool and smug, and he can definitely be kind of sharp, but he's actually really sweet. All marshmallow fluff on the inside."

He poked her on the forehead with his index finger. "You're. Crazy."

Keys rattled in the front door, and Dulcie startled awake with a shrill bark.

There was only one other person, according to Caroline, who had a key to this house. *Oh good*, thought Evan. *Here he is now.*

CHAPTER FOUR

Malcolm Umbertini came in bearing a large pizza box and six-pack of Rogue Hazelnut Brown, looking tall and urbanely gorgeous and not at all *sweet*, his trench coat spotted with rain, open over a navy suit.

"I'm here," he announced in his big baritone voice, as though reality hadn't just rearranged itself so that he was the center and focus of everything.

Maybe it was Caroline's ridiculous idea that Mal was interested in him that made Evan assess him with new eyes: his tall long-legged body, his purple-on-purple polka-dot tie, his face like that of an old movie star. All handsome cheekbones and lazy dark eyes, five-o'clock shadow on his jaw.

"What are we watching?" asked Mal, hanging up his raincoat. "Beefcake movies?"

"*Thor*," said Caroline.

"Thuper." Mal tossed the pizza onto the coffee table with a slap, and Dulcie emerged from beneath, spooked and wide-eyed. "Oh, I'm sorry," he said to her, addressing her exactly as he would a person. "I didn't mean to scare you." She went to him, sat by his knee, and he bent to scratch behind her ears. "You seem to be an intelligent animal," he told her, and she quivered with delight.

Mal straightened and went into the kitchen and began opening cabinets. He called, "Who wants a beer?"

Evan watched, disgruntled, as Dulcie happily followed him.

"I'm okay with tea," said Caroline.

Gathering his courage to try to talk and act like a normal person, Evan said, "I'll have one."

Mal came back into the living room, dealt out plates, handed Evan a cold bottle, and settled into the armchair across from them. Dulcie leaned on Mal's leg and gazed at him with unashamed adoration, which he seemed to accept as his due. Flipping open the pizza box, he said sternly, "I expect to see you eat an entire goddamn piece of pizza, Caro, do you hear me? Don't just nibble off the green peppers."

"I can eat without supervision, Mal," Caroline said, sliding a triangle of pizza onto her plate.

"Yeah, I've seen you," Mal softened his voice to mimic Caroline's. "'This slice has exactly three hundred and seventeen calories, so all I have to eat is two-fifths of it and four grapes to meet my daily dinner requirement—'"

Evan glared at Mal through narrow eyes. He was about to interrupt—*Do not food-shame my sister, you fucking asshole*—when Caroline jabbed him with an elbow. "I'm gonna say two thirty," she said, evaluating the piece of pizza in her hand. "So I can have a single grape too."

"Eat the pizza, Farkas," said Mal. "Oh, I forgot napkins." He got up and went back into the kitchen, either unaware of Evan's irritated stare or ignoring it.

"It's okay," Caroline said quietly. "He's known about the Food Game for years."

"He doesn't have to be such a jerk about it."

She elbowed him again, more gently this time. "He's not a jerk, he's covering up concern by acting like a dick. It's what we do, Boxy. Don't let it bug you."

Mal came back in with paper towels, and settled into a chair.

"How's your mom?" asked Caroline.

Malcolm rolled his eyes. "Saw her yesterday. She always wants to go to the same awful Chinese restaurant. It's like she'd rather complain about bad food than eat something good."

Caro said to Evan, "She's in assisted living in Troutdale."

"Really?" asked Evan, engaged despite himself. "Which one? Brookdale or Cedar Heights?"

"Cedar Heights," said Mal.

"That's where I work," said Evan. "What's her name?"

"Dorothy Wallace."

Evan put down his pizza. "Dorothy Wallace is your mother? Oh my God." He began to laugh. "You're *My son, the attorney*. Of course you are. I can totally see it."

Mal blinked at him. "I've never seen you there."

"You take her to dinner at Tsang's on Stark Street every Thursday night. I work an early shift on Thursdays, so I'm gone by the time you get there. But she tells us *all* about you on Friday mornings."

For the first time since Evan had met him, Mal looked genuinely thrown. "I'm sorry," he said, his eyebrows drawn together. "She can be kind of difficult."

"*Yeah*, she can," agreed Evan, grinning. "She threatens to try to have me fired at least once a week. She's one of my favorites."

Mal was staring at him with his brow crinkled. "Are you being sarcastic?"

"No," said Evan. "I really like her."

"Well," said Mal, "then I apologize in advance for the moment she figures out you're gay and calls you a pansy."

"Oh, she knows I'm gay. Assisted living is like the eye of a gossip hurricane. Everyone knows everything about everyone." Mal still seemed disconcerted, so Evan explained, "Okay. Assisted living can be humiliating for the residents. People get cranky. They lash out sometimes. It's normal, it's part of the job. But there was this one resident, a man, who kept complaining about the faggot nurse, and wanted to get some kind of special do-not-resuscitate order that only applied to me—so that any of the other nurses could help him if he was dying, but I couldn't? I mean, he was really just venting, but it was bad for everyone's morale. And then Dorothy got right in his face in the exercise room and told him to stop being such a miserable old coward. In front of all the other residents. It was awesome."

Mal stared at him for a long moment. "I'm sorry, but you're pissing me off. She and my dad threw me out and used my college fund to buy a summer house, but she defends *you* against homophobes?"

Evan grimaced, pulling his lips back from his teeth in a hiss of sympathy. "Maybe she grew up?"

"Maybe she did." Mal leaned back in his chair and picked up his slice of pizza.

So Mal wasn't just Caroline's handsome obnoxious friend; he was Dorothy Wallace's handsome complicated son, who took her to dinner once a week like clockwork, but never dropped by for a spontaneous visit. Who, according to Dorothy, could have made a lot of money in a big New York law firm, but had instead *"thrown himself away working for the county."*

And who had been badly hurt by her at some point, apparently. He tried to imagine being Dorothy Wallace's kid and suppressed a shudder—she was outspoken, sharp-tongued, completely lacking a sense of humor, and godawful opinionated. Reluctantly, he found himself liking Mal better, for trying to have a relationship with Dorothy in spite of everything.

"So," said Mal, changing the subject. "What were you two talking about when I came in?"

What? Oh, they'd been talking about *him*. Evan bit his tongue, but Caroline said smoothly, "Which Avenger is the hottest."

Mal's mouth curved up in his sardonic one-sided smile. His dark eyes rested on Evan. "And the verdict?"

"We hadn't really decided," said Caro. "There's a lot of hotness to choose from."

Mal raised his eyebrows at Evan.

"Uh. Well, *that's* pretty undeniable," Evan said, gesturing at Caroline's TV, where Chris Hemsworth was looking both cute and brawny in Viking armor and a cape.

"Movie Thor, mm, yes," agreed Mal, crossing his ankles. "Comics Thor is constantly saying things like 'By the bristling beard of Odin!' which I think detracts. What do you think, Caro?"

"I'm kind of into Tony Stark," she said.

Mal nodded judiciously, as he crunched into his pizza crust, and despite himself Evan was amused. "Who do you think is?"

Mal deliberately took a sip of his beer, set it down, then brushed his fingertips—a theatrical gesture that Evan imagined he used in court. "The hottest Avenger is Bucky Barnes, tragic antihero and coded gay icon. Completely miserable and vulnerable loaded with self-betrayal and angst. Plus he's gorgeous."

Evan smiled into his beer. Apparently Mal was a comics fan. All the markers of nerdery were there: the enthusiasm, the fascination with detail. It was funny.

Caro nudged Evan. "Which one is Bucky Barnes?"

"I dunno. Hang on." Evan fished his phone out of his pocket.

"Captain America's friend?" said Mal. "The Winter Soldier?"

"Oh, right. Yes. We haven't gotten to this one yet." Evan pulled up a movie still of Sebastian Stan, glowering sexily through his blowing hair, and handed it to Caro. "Solid choice."

He was echoing Mal's phrase from the other day, and Mal smiled at him—not the usual devious smirk but a wide, amused grin, all white teeth and sparkling eyes, as though Evan had just said something truly hilarious.

Ooof. You could get drunk off a smile like that. Evan looked away, hot and tight-chested from the full force of Mal's charisma.

"But Bucky's not an Avenger," said Caroline. "He's a villain. He's disqualified."

"He's Captain America's nemesis-slash-homoerotic bestie. You can't disqualify him," said Mal.

"If you can include a homoerotic bestie, I can include an X-Man, so the winner is clearly Patrick Stewart as Professor Xavier."

"Caro, the man is pushing eighty," protested Mal.

"Yes, and?"

"And you have daddy issues."

"Granted. Are you claiming you wouldn't do Patrick Stewart?" she challenged.

Mal seemed to soberly weigh the question for a moment. "If I could time-travel back to his Star Trek days, I would," he said regretfully. "X-Men Patrick Stewart . . . I have to admit I prefer them a little closer to my own age. What do you think, Doyle?"

"About Patrick Stewart?" repeated Evan. "I mean, Caroline's daddy issues are my daddy issues."

"Is that a yes?"

"Absolutely."

Mal laughed.

Oh God, I'm flirting with him. This is bad. Evan cast a helpless glance at his sister, who seamlessly rescued him. "Such a comics geek, Mal," she teased, as Evan concentrated on eating another slice of pizza and not being an idiot.

"When I was a kid, comics were my primary source of pictures of muscular men in skintight outfits," said Mal, smiling. "I cut them out and taped them to the walls of my room, while listening to Broadway cast recordings from the library. I cannot imagine why my parents persisted in thinking I was even remotely straight."

"Did they?" asked Evan, trying to reconcile this dweeby image with the urbane man before him.

"Yes, and I was the gayest child ever seen in Prince Frederick, Maryland. I tried to tell them but they denied it for *years*. It was like the Bataan Death March of coming out." Mal paused. "That's a tasteless metaphor, isn't it? Sorry. The something-long-and-agonizing of coming out. Anyway, they remained convinced that the right girl would eventually come along and turn me into a real boy, until they actually caught me. Having actual sex, with my actual boyfriend, in their actual kitchen, the night of my high school graduation party. Why are we talking about my mother again? Oh, comic books. Well. I'm told that there are pictures of women in comics too, but I don't remember any."

"Oo, listen to him talk," murmured Evan to Caroline.

"I know," she said, resting her head on his shoulder. "You should hear him when he's mad. He can strip the bark off trees."

"Was your family okay with the gay, Doyle?" asked Mal suddenly.

Evan hesitated, until Caro turned her eyes up to him. "I always knew, and Mom didn't care," she said. "Were you out at school?"

"Not really?" Evan fumbled for words. "It's not that it wasn't a big deal. It was. But not nearly as big a deal as, you know. Mom. Caroline and I were all about staying out of trouble, so that no one would ever ask questions, or notice what was up with her. So I didn't do a lot to call attention to myself. But I got with a couple boys in high school, and people knew. It helped that I was big for my age."

"The rest of the world seems to have caught up with you since then, hasn't it?" said Caroline.

"Shut up."

"And your mom didn't mind that you were gay?" asked Mal.

"She told me to be careful to not get AIDS, but other than that, nah."

"That's such a classic straight-person gesture of caring," said Mal. "*Don't get AIDS!*"

"Yeah. I think I said, 'Okay, Mom, I won't,' and that was the end of it." He shrugged. "Mom was a long-term heroin user. She wasn't exactly present a lot of the time."

That killed the conversation nicely. They watched *Thor*. Well, Evan and Mal watched *Thor*; Caro fell asleep on Evan's shoulder. At some point Mal got up to get himself another beer, and when he came back he sat on the couch beside Evan, rather than in the chair.

On the screen, Tom Hiddleston screamed, "Tell me!"

"Loki or Thor?" murmured Mal.

Evan kept his eyes on the TV, a smile tugging his mouth. The answer was obvious. Thor was blond, righteous, and wholesome. Loki was twisted and sinister. "Thor."

"Really? I think Loki all the way."

"No."

He felt Mal's laugh, a huff of breath on his ear. Then Mal's hand brushed his shoulder, the nape of his neck.

Evan jumped like he'd been stung by a wasp. He sat up, turning to give Mal an astonished stare. His sudden motion awakened Caroline. "What?" she mumbled sleepily.

"Nothing," said Evan, getting to his feet. "I'm going to take the dog outside. I think she needs to pee. Don't pause it."

"Doyle," said Mal.

Evan shook his head at him. "Stay."

Dulcie had awakened from a sound sleep at the magic words *the dog* and *outside*, and she stretched to her feet. Evan found his shoes and jacket, clicked his tongue to her, and went out the kitchen door into Caroline's backyard, closing the door firmly behind him.

He sat on the concrete steps in the wet darkness and watched Dulcie sniff her way appreciatively around the perennial border of Caroline's backyard.

The wind and blowing drizzle cooled his hot face. His heart beat loudly and steadily in his chest.

Mal had just come on to him.

It was exciting. Flattering, no doubt. Mal was tall, dark, and handsome. Smart, charming, smoking hot. Out, proud, well-dressed.

He had a worthwhile career, a sense of humor, and a glow of self-confidence like a heat mirage rippling off him. He topped (Evan was certain), and did it well. This town had to be full of guys eager to let him. He was exactly the type of hot asshole that Evan had always found attractive, had always instinctively shied away from.

To think that he might throw a pass to *Evan*, of all people?

Mal Umbertini was Relationship Material. The kind of man you introduced to your family, made long-term plans with.

Evan Doyle was *not* Relationship Material. He was Occasional Hookup Material at best. Evan had stopped being fit for guys like Mal a long, long time ago. In fact, Mal wasn't just out of his league; they weren't even playing the same game.

Dulcie did her business and then picked up an empty plastic water bottle someone had chucked in the corner of the yard. She bounced to Evan, wagging her tail, and dropped it at his feet.

"Found a toy, huh?" He tossed the bottle and she leaped to catch it in midair, then performed a dance of triumph, shaking the plastic bottle, crunching it in her jaws, before returning it to him. He played fetch with her for a while, letting the dog's uncomplicated joy, and the cool night, calm him.

What Mal wanted didn't matter. Though he apparently didn't see the impossibility of the thing, it was blinking like a neon sign before Evan's eyes.

And that was *fine*. Evan was a defective former hustler, but after all, that wasn't all he was. He also had a career, salaried with benefits, and a home, and friends, and a newfound sister. There was nothing wrong with his life. Nothing missing that he needed. He did okay, he and his fellow Occasional Hookups.

And if that idea made him feel a little depressed, well, no one needed to know but himself, Dulcie, and the rain.

The door behind him opened and Mal came out, wearing his raincoat. Before Evan could say anything he said, "Caro's boyfriend, Paul, just showed up."

"Shit," said Evan, standing up. "I thought he was busy tonight. Does he know about me?"

"I don't think so," said Mal. "And he doesn't need to know you were ever here, if you don't want."

"I don't."

"Okay. She's distracting him so you can get away. Do you have everything?"

"Yeah." Evan whistled for Dulcie and then snapped a leash onto her harness. "I'll go."

He let himself out the back gate. Somewhat to his surprise, Mal said, "Doyle, wait," and came with him. "I wanted to apologize for earlier. For touching you. I didn't mean to send you flying out the window."

Evan didn't know how to respond. He couldn't find the middle ground between *I did* not *fly out the window* and *Don't ever touch me again*. So he just shook his head.

They walked, Dulcie tapping along ahead of them at the end of her leash. As usual, Evan kept his eyes on the dog. Her senses were sharper than his. If they were approached—if they were watched—Dulcie would know. She was no guard dog, but her body language would alert him to any threat.

But Dulcie was relaxed, sniffing along happily at the end of her leash. Evan, to distract himself from the jittery prickling at the nape of his neck, asked, "So do you like Paul?"

Mal snorted softly.

"That bad?"

"Oh, he's fine," said Mal. "I've seen worse. But Caro doesn't really waste her time with guys who might stick around, so it tends to be a parade of cheats and deadbeats, and other such losers."

It was not unlike Evan's life, though "parade" implied greater numbers than existed. But it seemed sadder that Caroline chose to live that way than that he did. Surely Kiki deserved better than the kinds of dregs he scraped by on.

He turned down Hawthorne toward his truck, Mal keeping pace beside him, raincoat flapping in the breeze.

"You don't have to walk me to my car," Evan said.

"I live in one of those brick things up there," said Mal, pointing to a development of new-looking town houses a few blocks ahead. "I'm not walking you to your car; you're walking me home."

Mal's warm tone made Evan a little flushed and dizzy. Mal was doing it again. Smiling at him, walking too close. Charming him.

Walking down the street with him felt like a dangerous and exciting adventure. He needed to tell Caroline to be his chaperone. *Don't leave me alone with Mal again*, he'd say to her. *I like it too much.*

With gratitude he reached his truck. He unlocked the passenger door and gestured to Dulcie, who hopped into the cab.

"Can I buy you another beer?" asked Mal, nodding toward a bar on the corner. "Or a soda, since you're driving?"

"Uh, thanks, no."

"Or you could come have a drink at my place."

Goddamn it.

So tempting. All the rainy self-pep-talks in the world didn't make that offer, now it had come, any less appetizing. He could tell himself that he didn't want Mal, but there he was, looking at him with glowing dark eyes. Evan met those eyes, and acknowledged the promise of Mal's slim long-limbed body, that full-lipped mouth.

Mal's eyes brightened. A corner of his mouth curled.

"It's not a good idea," said Evan.

"It's a *great* idea."

Should I? No. Yes. *No.* He couldn't. "Too complicated."

"Maybe I like complicated." Mal's voice had gone growly.

"Maybe I don't." Then Evan climbed behind the wheel of his truck, closed the door firmly, and started the ignition. Mal stepped back as he drove away.

All the long drive home, Evan's body felt half-aroused and half-alarmed. He focused on the road and ignored the prickling heat rushing through his veins.

Like he'd had a close escape. Or a missed opportunity.

CHAPTER FIVE

"**S**o, what does your family think of your choice of career?"

Evan glanced up to see the contemptuous set of his patient's jaw. It was Monday morning, at Cedar Heights, and he was gently peeling a pad of bandages from Mr. Willison's shin.

Last week Mr. Willison had banged his leg against the corner of a coffee table. His eighty-year-old skin had torn and produced an impressive gout of blood, and he'd fainted. He'd been a bear ever since, unpleasant to staff and his fellow residents alike. Evan supposed the old man had felt ashamed and frightened that such a minor mishap could cause such a gigantic disruption to his life.

And now he was mad about it.

"I'm an orphan." Evan stripped off his gloves, washed his hands, dried them, and put on new gloves. "This is healing up nice."

"An orphan?"

"My mother died when I was a teenager."

"And your father?"

"Not around too much." He began to clean the wound, careful not to pull on the stitches. "How's the pain? Is this keeping you awake at night?"

"It's fine," said Mr. Willison, brusquely. "Where was your father? Why wasn't he there for you?"

"You'd have to ask him." Evan patted Mr. Willison's leg dry. "First you'd have to find him. I never met the guy."

"Huh," said Mr. Willison. "They say that an overbearing mother, and an absent father, can cause . . ."

Evan met Mr. Willison's eyes, and the old man trailed off, not quite rude enough to finish that sentence right to Evan's face.

Mr. Willison is not trying to be a dick, Evan reminded himself, beginning to wrap clean gauze around the wound. He was probably as much a product of his upbringing as Evan was. Pinned like a bug to his ideas about masculinity, he likely could not get his mind around the idea that Evan might accept himself.

So Evan gave him a smile. "I've heard that too," he said peacefully.

"Maybe if you'd gone into the Scouts," said Mr. Willison. "Or sports. Found a strong male influence."

Evan probably failed to hide his amusement. "I have to admit, it's really not something that I worry about."

"Why *not?*"

"It's just the way it is. Honestly, being gay is the least of my worries." He patted the old man's leg, then tugged the cuff of his US Army sweatpants down over the bandage, restoring his dignity as much as possible. "I'm pleased with how well this is healing, but if the pain gets worse, or if it starts to feel hot, or you feel sick to your stomach, you have to let one of us know right away, okay?"

Mr. Willison huffed. In Evan's professional opinion, he would no more let them know if his symptoms worsened than he would kiss Evan on the mouth. They'd have to watch him like a hawk.

"You ready to go down to lunch? Smells like stew today."

Evan typed up his notes in Mr. Willison's file, then got his own lunch and retired to the privacy of the nurses' office to eat. Stew, cornbread, tomato and cucumber salad, iced tea: probably about three hundred fifty calories. He'd just opened his book of crosswords to work on a puzzle while he ate when his cell phone rang. Normally he'd ignore it while at work, but it was Caroline.

"Hello."

"Hey, Boxy, can you hear us all right? Mal and I are on speaker phone."

"Oh," he said. "Hi."

"Hi," said Mal, his voice a little echoey. "We have news."

Awkward. Evan's usual modus, upon rejecting or being rejected, was to fade right out of the life of the other party. That was not going to be possible with his sister's best friend. "Oh," he said again. "I'm going to eat while you tell me what's up, if that's okay? It's my lunch hour."

"Perfect," said Mal. And to Caroline: "Should I go first, or you?"

"You go," she said.

"Right," said Mal briskly. "We divvied up the research, Doyle. I got Pablo Ramón Icaza, late of El Centro, California."

Evan put down his spoon, annoyed. "You did what? Why?"

Caroline said, "Oh please, Boxy. You knew we'd dig."

Well, shit. He should have known. How far had she gone? How much had she found out? "You knew I'd tell you what I wanted you to know," he snapped.

"Yeah, well, you've been pretty quiet for the last decade and a half," said Caroline, bluntly, "so I'm digging."

Mal's voice, quieter. "You said he wouldn't mind."

"He doesn't mind," scoffed Caroline. "He's just not used to it."

Yes, I mind. He gritted his teeth. It wasn't that he didn't intend to tell Caroline everything. She had a right to know, and he didn't want secrets between them. But it was *hard*. She should know that it was too hard to vomit up every painful thing all at once. She should know that he needed a little time.

Naïve of him though, to imagine that she would wait. If she hadn't learned everything already, she would.

He pressed a hand to his stomach, willing his surge of terror to subside. He didn't have to be afraid of Caroline.

"Boxy, it's good news," Caroline was saying. "Don't you want to hear what we found out?"

"Go on," he growled.

"Okay," said Mal. "Pablo Ramón Icaza used to control all the meth traffic in southern California and Arizona, and was getting ready to move on Vegas, when your evidence got him arrested, and he threatened to have a lot of unpleasant things done to you."

"I remember," said Evan. *"I'll burn him alive and piss on his ashes"* had been one of the threats. The prosecutors had been very anxious about Icaza. Evan . . . Evan had been anxious about everything.

"Much of his organization was arrested at the same time," said Mal, "including the US Border Patrol agent who was helping move product in from Mexico, and the banker in Los Angeles who was his money launderer. Both of them rolled on Icaza, and more threats were made. The banker's evidence, in particular, nailed the lid on Icaza's coffin, and from what most people can tell, Icaza's wrath transferred to him. After he gave evidence, all the threats were against this banker. Doyle, stop me if you know all of this, okay?"

"I was probably told a lot of it at the time, but the details are a little fuzzy." He'd struggled with constant depression and anxiety, those first few years. His foster parents had been stern. They'd scheduled his days and nights to the second: homework sessions, doctor's appointments, therapy, cooking lessons, exercise. He remembered them with gratitude, because he undoubtedly owed them his life, but he'd found them incredibly stifling. "Had a lot of drama. Didn't really pay attention."

Mal continued, "A price was put on the banker's head. He went into witness protection too. About ten years ago someone found him and took a shot at him, and they had to transfer him. Anyway, as far as anyone can tell, Icaza and his people forgot about you and focused on the banker."

"As far as anyone can tell," said Evan.

"Yes. And then Icaza died in prison. Cirrhosis of the liver. He'd picked up hepatitis C somewhere. I talked to a guy in the DEA, and he says that all the bits and dribs of Icaza's gang have been rolled up into someone else's organization now, and they've all moved on to the next chapter in their lives. No one is after the banker anymore. He's been living openly under his old name for years. No one even remembers you. My DEA guy says you could go back to being you anytime you want." He could hear Mal's encouraging smile, even through the phone. He sounded pleased to be able to tell Evan this, and clearly expected him to be pleased to hear it.

Evan silently ate some stew, mopped up the bottom of his bowl with his bread, considering how to respond. The first words that came to his lips—*None of this helps me*—seemed ungrateful and mean.

Because it was good news. Evan was glad that no one had murdered Icaza's money guy; he was glad to know that no one was still hunting for him.

But this whole conversation brought up so many bad memories, the kinds of memories that sometimes circled around and around in his mind at night, keeping him from rest. That incessant gnawing worry wasn't based in reality, and Mal's news wasn't going to resolve it.

"Thanks," he said flatly.

Caroline said, "My job was to look into John Nesbit Everett."

Evan pushed his food away, his stomach clenching. *Here we go.* "Maybe this could wait for another time."

"No," she said inexorably. "This is good stuff. Listen."

"Caroline—"

"*Listen.* Everett was arrested at about the same time as Icaza. Not for the murder of Derrick Sanders and Kimberly Farkas, which is why I've never heard of him, but for an extravagant collection of drug charges."

Yeah, Evan would need to talk to her about that sometime. Soon.

She went on, "He pled guilty to possession, manufacture, and trafficking of a schedule-two controlled substance, and under California's three-strikes law was convicted of twenty-five years in prison. But," she went on, "since the state of California also deemed him a nonviolent offender, he got early release six years ago, due to overcrowding."

Nez is out? Evan wrapped his arms around his stomach and put his forehead down on his desk. "Caroline," he said weakly.

She might not have heard him, because she went on. "He immediately went to Reno to get his party on. There he hooked up with Emily Trammell, a college student who also did a little sex work on the side. Sounds like it started consensual, but when it was time for her to go home, Everett refused to let her go. He bound her and transported her across state lines to Sacramento—"

"Stop." Evan dropped the phone. "Stop. Stop."

Dulcie was now in his lap. He hugged her, rocking, eyes squeezed shut.

Oh God, oh God. Emily Trammell. A college student. A girl who'd had no idea what she'd been getting into.

Voices tinny through the phone, Mal and Caroline were arguing.

"What the fuck is the matter with you?" Mal was demanding. "He is the victim of a crime, and you talk to him like that." Evan couldn't make out what Caroline said, but it sounded defensive. Mal snapped, "Oh, hell, Caro. On your worst day you are better than this."

An obscure impulse to shield his sister made him pick up the phone again. Blotting sweat off his face with his sleeve, he said,

"I'm still here. Caroline." He gulped for breath. "Caroline. In what universe is any of that good stuff?"

Her tone was now conciliatory. "The point is that he broke federal law, Boxy. And now he's in a high-security federal prison, and will be for the rest of his life. No parole, no good behavior, no early release. Not for any reason."

He breathed hard through his nose; his eyes were running. After a moment, he asked, "Was she okay?"

A pause on the other end of the phone. Maybe they hadn't expected that question.

"She was hurt," Caroline said. "But as far as I know she's okay now. She graduated with a degree in communications and moved away. Put it behind her."

"Can you get me her address?" He couldn't keep the bitterness out of his voice when he added, "Since you're so good at *research*?"

"I'll try," she said. "Boxy . . . I just wanted you to know. He didn't go to prison for killing Mom and Derrick, but he *is* in prison."

Furious, cornered, Evan snarled, "Nez didn't go to prison for killing Mom and Derrick because he didn't kill Mom and Derrick."

There was a shocked silence.

"What?" Caro's voice had gone sharp with bewilderment. "He didn't? Then who—"

"Okay, whoa," interrupted Mal. "Let's not do this on the phone."

That was the smartest fucking thing anyone had said all day. "Let's not," Evan agreed. "Don't call me at work again, not unless it's an emergency. I've got people who depend on me. I need to keep my shit together."

"We thought you'd want to know right away," said Mal. "That you're safe from both these guys. So you don't need to worry anymore."

"It doesn't work that way," said Evan, and hung up.

CHAPTER SIX

Mal didn't give himself too much time to dwell on Evan Doyle. As one of Multnomah County's less-senior prosecutors, it was part of his job to unclog the judicial drains: grand jury sessions, hearings, and reams of paperwork for the unending stream of crimes that flowed beneath Portland's peaceful and leafy surface. Misdemeanor assault, public indecency, unlawful possession, harassment, burglary, providing false information to a public safety officer, driving under the influence, identity theft. The more of these he could close, quickly and without trial, the more resources could be devoted to nastier, knottier items. And he had some of those on his plate too—a schoolteacher caught with weird porn on his work computer. A violent kidnap/rape. A heartbreaking child-abuse case.

So he kept busy. But it would be a lie to say that Evan Doyle was ever far from his mind.

Evan Doyle, whose façade bristled with defenses; whose eyes were haunted with mysteries. Mal wanted to know everything, solve his problems, ease his hurts, fuck him into next week. All of which was ridiculous. Evan's face was beautiful and his body was delicious, but he was so taut with mistrust and old pain that it was hard to imagine him making himself vulnerable enough to let Mal in, let alone have sex.

Although, a couple of times at Caro's place, a genuine smile had broken through, spontaneous and easy. Once in a while Evan relaxed. When that happened, Mal couldn't help but picture him. Sweaty and unrestrained with pleasure. Would he be shy in bed? Would he yield control to his partner? Or would he be demanding, aggressive? Mal could spend all day pondering those questions.

"I don't think you have much of a chance," Caro had reported. *"I'm sorry, Mal. He wouldn't even consider it."*

Not *quite* true. Evan had considered it. For perhaps two glorious seconds, Evan Doyle had looked at Mal and considered it.

He'd then turned Mal down with a thoroughness that hadn't left a whole lot of room for hope. And after that, there had been that blunder of a phone call.

But Mal remembered those two seconds, and hoped.

On Thursday after work, Mal went to the gym for his daily swim, then showered and headed out to Troutdale for his weekly date with his mother. Cedar Heights provided its well-heeled residents with private apartments, garden balconies, and discreet call buttons in case of emergency. Housekeeping staff cleaned up after them and did their laundry; a restaurant-style dining hall provided nutritionally balanced and reasonably tasty meals. There was a gym and a pool and a movie theater and a daily roster of healthful activities, and nursing staff were on hand at all hours to help manage meds and deal with the accumulating symptoms of old age.

Mal could acknowledge that Cedar Heights was quite nice, all things considered, while admitting to himself that the place gave him the creeps.

As he walked through the lobby, he couldn't help glancing around at the staff. Of course Evan wouldn't be here; he didn't work Thursday evenings.

But when Mal passed by the RN office on the way to the elevator, there he was.

On Thursday evenings, that office was usually inhabited by a cheerful young woman named Jackie, buxomly overflowing her blue scrubs. Today it was Evan in the blue scrubs, perched on a rolling stool, examining the forearm of an elderly woman. She was talking, and he nodded while he rolled up the sleeve of her sweater. He seemed relaxed and confident.

And so he should be: Evan looked great. As before, both his wrists were encircled by black bands—one wristwatch, one leather bracelet—and the fluorescent light of the RN station brought out amber highlights in his rough brown hair. He'd layered the blue scrub top over a long-sleeved navy Henley and jeans, and he made it look fucking good.

Mal shook off the impulse to stop and say hello, and pushed the Up button on the elevator. He was here to see his mom, not crush on the staff. Plus, Evan's response earlier in the week, when Mal and Caro had called him, had made it clear that he didn't welcome intrusions while he was working.

Dorothy Stirling Umbertini Wallace met Mal at her apartment door and took his arm for the walk back down to the car. She didn't move too quickly anymore, and sometimes got worryingly short of breath, although she appeared much more youthful than her seventy-one years. That was partly due to her excellent taste in clothes: she always dressed with an understated elegance that only money could buy. Today she wore a green tweed skirt suit, and as usual her only jewelry was two handsome diamond engagement rings, one from each of her deceased husbands.

"Where shall we go for dinner?" he asked her, helping her into the passenger seat of his car.

"The usual."

The usual was Tsang's, a restaurant that served hubcap-sized platters of bland, surely-this-can't-be-authentic Chinese food. Every entrée was accompanied by a softball-sized scoop of fried rice, gleaming with grease and dotted with peas and cubes of ham. Portions were so large and unappetizing they usually shared one. Mom claimed that she liked their sesame shrimp.

She'd had plenty of time to get used to it. A few years ago she had called Mal out of the blue, after almost a decade's total estrangement, to tell him that she had moved across the country to Troutdale to be near him, her only child, and would he like to have dinner? She'd suggested Tsang's in what he'd interpreted as a sign of disdain for his income.

"Are you sure you wouldn't like to try something different?"

She looked at him down her nose, with refined puzzlement. "No, why?"

He sighed and drove to Tsang's.

His feelings for her since then were a tangle of resentment and obligation and grudging respect. And he loved her, of course. He wasn't sure he liked her very much, and he certainly didn't trust her with anything but the most superficial information about his life, but he did somehow love her.

They ordered and were waiting for their meal when Dorothy said, "Malcolm, I have a surprise for you." She pulled a small wrapped box out of her alligator handbag and passed it to him over the dinner table.

"I wasn't expecting a gift," he said, coolly accepting it.

"Naturally not," she said, with nearly equal coolness. "It's a surprise."

He reluctantly untied the shiny ribbon.

She often gave him surprise gifts. This time it was a pair of cuff links: round, dark-blue enamel with brushed silver rims.

"These will match your navy suit," she said.

Turning the cool metal studs over in his fingers, he bit the inside of his cheek. Last month it had been a silk tie. He wrestled with an impulse to reject them, to tell her to stop spending money on him. He was an adult with a perfectly adequate salary, and he could buy his own goddamn cuff links.

Perhaps it would be easier to be gracious if she gave him tacky gifts. Perhaps then he could accept with a smile, and then toss them aside without a thought. But her gifts were always attractive, tasteful, and probably quite expensive. The cuff links would in fact look perfect with his navy suit.

"They're beautiful," he said stiffly. "Thank you."

The waitress arrived to plunk down their plates of food and refilled their teacups. Mal put the box aside and changed the subject. "I met someone who works at Cedar Heights last week. I guess he's a nurse there. His name's Evan Doyle?"

"Oh yes, he's one of the RNs," said his mother. "How did you meet?"

"We were introduced by a mutual friend," said Mal. "We had pizza and talked."

She looked pleased. "He's a very intelligent young man. Last month Gloria Anderson went all loopy, and it was Evan who figured out that there was a problem with her drugs."

Dorothy launched into a long story that brutally condemned the incompetence of Gloria Anderson's physicians, not to mention the uncaring blindness of her children and grandchildren. Eventually she worked her way back to "But Evan figured it out and made them get a second opinion. If he hadn't, they'd probably have moved her into a dementia home, so I really think that doctor should be sued."

"Well, good," said Mal, when he could get a word in. "I'm glad the staff there know what they're doing."

"I told Evan that he's wasted in a place like that," Dorothy said illogically. "He should go back to school and become a doctor."

At least once a week she told Mal that he was wasted at the district attorney's office and should go to work for a private law firm. "What did he say?"

"He said he didn't care for golf."

Mal laughed, and Dorothy said waspishly, "I hardly see what that has do with anything. Was it a date?"

Mal blinked at this unexpected conversational swerve. "What?"

"You and Evan, eating pizza. Was it a date?"

She didn't have a right to ask questions like that. Mal surveyed his mother across a gulf, made up of years of silence and anger and unspoken accusations.

They had never discussed the catastrophic confrontation that had driven him furiously away from home, into the arms of a new life. He hadn't seen or spoken to his father again; he hadn't been invited to his funeral, nor to her wedding to her second husband, whom he'd never met. She had never apologized or explained. He'd never apologized—didn't even know if she wanted him to—and had never offered to forgive her. She did frequently nag him about being single, but this was the first time she'd acknowledged that, if he weren't single, he'd be with a man.

"No," he said, feeling like he was tiptoeing through a minefield. "I don't think Evan would be interested in dating me."

"Of course he'd be interested. You're an *attorney*." Mal had never exactly found this to be a relationship slam dunk, but didn't say so; she pressed on. "Evan lives all by himself in a little cabin in the boonies, with no neighbors. I'm sure he's lonely. You should ask him."

It was weird, because Mal was not accustomed to his mother's wishes aligning with his own. But that was exactly what he wanted to do. He wanted to *ask* Evan. To court him with gifts and compliments and tokens of esteem. He wanted to woo him, and gain his trust, and win him. He felt like a suitor, and Evan a damsel in a tower.

He smiled at his mother. "Should I?"

"Why not?"

He turned that question over in his mind. Why not? Because, for one thing, Evan was no maiden, but a vigorous adult male who didn't need Mal's rescuing arms. Whose brawny physique suggested that he could, in fact, beat the shit out of a limp-wristed nerd like Mal, if he were so inclined.

All the better. Because Mal had felt this way once before, about a man with a strong body and vulnerable eyes. A boy, really—they'd both been boys. And it had ended in disaster. Mal hadn't just grieved, he'd felt thrown away and worthless, his belief in himself shattered. For years, he'd felt that his love must be a futile thing, not worth having.

But he was no longer a boy. He knew that sometimes the world was cruel, but sometimes people loved in spite of that. And Evan was not Zach.

Mal was a little worried about the bracelets on Evan's wrists, though. Zach had mastered makeup techniques to conceal the parallel lines that patterned his forearms. Perhaps the leather bands on Evan's wrists covered up old wounds. Or new ones?

"You've been alone for a long time," said Dorothy, ignoring or not noticing his introspection. "It's nice to have someone. I won't always be here for you, Malcolm."

Mal was a professional arguer, but—as was so often true with his mother's conversational sallies—he was at a loss for how to respond to that.

After dinner was mercifully over, Mal drove his mother back to Cedar Heights, and was walking her up to her apartment as usual when they spotted Evan in the dining room. He was propping up a wall, ankles crossed, chatting with another blue-scrubbed staff person. To Mal's horror, his mother seized the bit between her teeth and marched into the dining room. Evan's relaxed pose vanished, while the other staff member saw them coming and evaporated. Trailing behind her, Mal heard Dorothy say, "Evan, you didn't tell me that you'd met my son!"

Evan looked wary, though as his gaze flickered between Mal and Dorothy, there was amusement there too.

Sorry, Mal mouthed, mortified, over her shoulder.

"He always takes me to Tsang's on Thursday nights," Dorothy was saying. "It's really not a very good restaurant, but he works for the *county*. He told me you and he went out to get pizza?"

"Uh, yes," said Evan, ignoring the inaccuracy of this, not to mention the obvious "date" implications. "Last week."

"Did you find you had much in common?" asked Dorothy coquettishly.

"We—uh—" Evan's eyes darted to him, widened with mock horror, then went back to Dorothy. "Malcolm told me all about his comic book collection."

"Oh, Malcolm just loved his comic books when he was a boy. He had several subscriptions, and when they came in the mail, he grabbed them and ran straight up to his room. He would disappear for the whole afternoon."

Mal face-palmed, then met Evan's eyes through his parted fingers. Evan was clearly trying not to laugh.

Dorothy sailed past the embarrassed pause. "Well! I'm tired. I'm going up. Evan, Malcolm wants to talk to you about my care. He was *so* worried when he heard about poor Gloria Anderson, and he wanted to ask about my medications. You two should talk. Mal, I'll see you next week."

As she marched away, Evan breathed, "Setup city."

"I'm really so, so sorry," said Mal. "I swear I wouldn't ask her to do something like this."

"Oh, I know. I recognize an original Dorothy Wallace impulse when I see one." Evan was laughing openly now, thank God.

"Usually a different RN is here on Thursdays."

"Jackie's kid has chicken pox, so I'm filling in." He was looking down at his hands, still smiling a little politely.

Do not stalk a man in his workplace. Mal began easing his way toward the exit. "Oh. Well, anyway. I'd better go. Nice to see you again, Doyle."

"Uh, before you go," said Evan, kicking off from the wall, "I've got some questions for you. About the law. And our conversation the other day. Could we—"

Yes, yes, yes! "Sure," said Mal, glancing at one of the empty tables.

"Oh, not here," said Evan. "This is Gossip Central Station. I get off work in about fifteen minutes, though. At nine. Maybe we could meet somewhere?"

Evan's hands were in the pockets of his jeans, his body closed off and turned slightly away from Mal's. His tone was brisk. Conclusion: not flirting. He seemed to actually have some questions. About the *law*. But this was an unforeseen golden opportunity. "Why don't you meet me at that bar on Hawthorne, right next to where you parked your truck the other night?" suggested Mal. "It's a Thursday night. It'll be quiet."

"Okay." Evan nodded casually. "Meet you there."

Mal did not give in to his grin and triumphant fist-pump until he got back to his car.

CHAPTER SEVEN

T he bar was called Pettygrove's, and at 9:10 on a Thursday night it was indeed relatively empty. They were playing Joy Division on the sound system, but that wasn't enough to douse Mal's excitement. He ordered his favorite porter and secured a booth.

Of course, if Evan really wanted to ask questions about the law, he needed Mal to be dispassionate. But Mal could no longer pretend to lawyerly dispassion: he found Evan fascinating.

He texted Caro.

E is meeting me for a beer, and I think he wants to pick my brain, but I'm so happy. Talk me down.

What does he want? she replied.

Advice about the law?

So not a date then.

Unfortunately, no.

After a few moments, she texted back, *Just listen. Let him reveal as much as he wants. Don't interrogate.*

With his thumbs he tapped out, *Teach your grandma to suck eggs.*

If he's not okay, tell me?

I will.

Joy Division made way for The Cure, which was replaced by the Eurythmics. "Blue Savannah" by Erasure filled him with sadness and the memory of a blue-eyed boy who he'd have followed anywhere, who had left him behind. Three hits of the eighties later, and Mal was seriously considering asking them to change the station. He was also wondering if he'd been stood up: Evan was late. Then Evan Doyle came in, his dog in her service vest at his heels.

He found Mal with a glance, nodded fractionally, and then went to the bar, where he gestured to the dog and got a nod from the bartender. As he walked over to Mal's table with a glass of beer in his hand, Mal appreciated the view. Evan had lost the scrubs but not the bracelet, and was looking good, the Henley shirt stretched nicely across his shoulders.

"Doyle," said Mal in greeting.

"Umbertini."

Evan sat down across from Mal while Dulcie insinuated herself into the space under the table. After a moment's hesitation, he raised his eyes.

Mal was struck again by the clarity of Evan's emotional expression. Evan said nothing, but he was an open book: his posture, his lucent eyes, the muscle working in his jaw, all communicated discomfort. According to Caro, Evan was shy, but he was clearly determined to be here in spite of his nervousness.

Maybe Mal's long wait had been due to that shyness. Maybe Evan had been sitting in his truck outside, trying to nerve himself to come in. So different from Zach, who used to sweep into every situation with élan, giving the appearance of complete fearlessness. Mal hadn't noticed that the fearlessness had been a mask.

"What are you drinking?" Mal asked, casually.

"IPA."

"Nasty," he said. "IPA is too bitter for me."

"I like nasty things," said Evan. Then he winced. "I mean, bitter things. I mean. Foods."

Mal smiled. He and Caro had been educated and trained to speak with crystal clarity. Trial work, debate; Caro had even gone to Toastmasters for a few years, to school herself out of the vocal mannerisms that Evan displayed. That hesitant Southern California drawl, the slight stammer. The not-perfectly-chosen words. Mal found it charming.

They chatted about beer a little, and Evan seemed to relax. After a few minutes Mal ventured, "Are you going to go back to your real name? You could, you know. It doesn't seem like there's any danger."

"No, I . . ." Evan's eyes were hooded. "I know. But I don't feel like Alex anymore. This never felt like an alias, really. It felt like . . . like I was different. A different person." He sipped his beer. "It's hard to explain."

Mal might understand better than Evan realized.

Evan added, "I can probably stop jumping down Caroline's throat when she calls me Alex, though." He glanced up with a slight smile, and in the dim bar his eyes were the color of slate. He said, "When you called. The information you gave me."

"Uh-huh."

"There's something I've kind of always wondered. I didn't know anyone I could ask before."

"Go on," said Mal.

A long pause. Evan stared at his beer. A little reluctantly, Mal said, "If you'd feel more comfortable asking Caro . . ."

Evan shook his head. "I don't want to upset her."

"She knows as much about criminal law as I do, if not more. And she's tough."

"I know. It's sort of easier with someone who doesn't know me. She— I know she deserves to know. You can tell her. It just gets so intense when I try to talk to her."

"Okay."

"Okay." Evan took a steadying breath, his forearms on the table. "So when I was sixteen. The cops raided the house where I was living. In El Centro."

"I remember. You were still sixteen?"

"Yes."

"So this was right after what happened at the En."

"Oh, yeah. Like . . . two weeks later."

"Okay."

"So. The cops raided the place. And . . . and it would have been pretty clear that I wasn't there voluntarily. Also, like I said, I was a minor."

Evan seemed composed, his voice low and clear—none of the horror and panic that had been there on the phone three nights ago showed on his face. But he kept his eyes down.

Mal considered what Evan was telling him, underneath his words. Considered the image of a much younger, smaller Evan, trapped and hurt, with no one to help him. For two weeks.

"Like Emily from Reno," he clarified.

"A lot like Emily from Reno. But, um, as you found out, Nez was only charged with the drug stuff. He went to prison for drug charges. Possession, manufacturing." Slowly, he raised his eyes, met Mal's. "Not for what he did to me. There was nothing on his record to tell what else he did. To me. He was considered a nonviolent offender. And I was wondering why, as a prosecutor, you would decide to do that. To not charge someone with that."

Mal sipped his beer for a moment, conscious of his heartbeat.

Evan was still looking at him, and Mal was braced by the glint in his eyes. Evan didn't want his sympathy; he wanted answers. Evan was no longer a terrified child. In fact, he looked angry.

Mal had been quiet for a while now, and Evan tipped his head slightly, much the way Caro did when she was questioning. "Do you understand what I'm asking?"

"I do," said Mal. "I'm just trying to figure out how to answer."

"With the truth?"

"I don't know the truth." Mal fidgeted with his beer glass, making rings of condensation on the table. Evan needed dispassion from him, not horror or pity. "I don't have your case file in front of me. I can only guess what the prosecutors in your case were thinking."

"And do you have a guess?"

"I'm guessing that maybe, at least in part, they were trying to spare you."

This was clearly not the answer Evan was expecting. He blinked at Mal, then blew out a sigh and leaned back in the booth. "How?"

Mal had talked to a lot of crime victims over the years, and he'd always found that the best approach was a straightforward one: plain talk, no euphemisms, no evasions. Evan wasn't just a crime victim to him, but the approach should be the same.

"Stop me if I'm wrong," he said briskly, "but charges they could have brought against Nez would include kidnapping, imprisonment, rape or statutory rape or lewd acts on a minor . . . That sort of thing. Is that more or less correct?"

"More or less," agreed Evan, putting a razor edge on that phrase.

Mal cleared his throat. "So, think of criminal law as a kind of game. Not because it's fun or funny, but because there are rules and opponents. Both sides present evidence according to very strict rules, and the jury decides which side wins, according to the rules as presented by the judge. Right?"

"Okay."

So far, so obvious. Mal cleared his throat, ticked points off his fingers. "Evidence. There's evidence from the house. Witness testimony from whoever saw you there. Medical evidence from your body. And your testimony. Prosecutors use all that evidence to present a picture of what happened. The defense's job is to make the jury doubt all that evidence and discredit the prosecution's account."

"I understand," said Evan.

"So where does the defense attorney start? You said that you were arrested."

"I was," said Evan. "Even though I was all busted up and . . . I thought, at the time, that the cops just saw gross homo activity, and didn't care about the details." He looked warily at Mal, perhaps thinking that, as a prosecutor, Mal would necessarily side with the police.

"I don't doubt it for a second," said Mal. "Were there drugs in your system when you were arrested?"

"Yes."

"So defense has evidence that you're a user, and he's got cops who're going to testify to gross homo activity."

"What does that have to do with anything?" protested Evan, his voice coldly incredulous. "I was zip-tied to a bed. I had deep-tissue bruises from having been beaten, and Nez made me take the drugs. I was *sixteen*."

Jesus Christ. Suddenly it was clearer why Evan was asking *Mal* this question, and not his sister.

"Doyle, I'm not trying to defend what the prosecutors in your case did," said Mal. "I'm presenting a possible scenario. I don't know why they did it, and I'm not saying they were right to do it."

Evan took a deep breath and rubbed his hands over his face. "I'm sorry. Okay."

"You don't have to be sorry," said Mal. "But you don't know how ugly this kind of trial can get until you've seen it. Defense will cast doubt on prosecution's account of what happened by trying to change the jury's perception of *who you are*. He starts by trying to make sure that the jury is a bunch of homophobes. He puts the asshole cops on the stand. He gets the drug evidence admitted. He uses the evidence that he has to paint a picture of you as a tough little methed-up hustler."

Evan had gone paler than usual; his beer was untouched.

Mal pushed on. "Maybe defense gets hold of some of Derrick's old buddies. They testify about what they paid for in the En."

Huskily, Evan said, "Did Caroline tell you about what they paid for in the En?"

"No. I guessed. Am I wrong?"

"No."

"So, that comes out in court. Maybe defense drags poor old Manuel Hernandez out of his straight life to talk about how you knew just what you were doing, back in high school. Those zip ties? The defense can't come right out and tell the jury that fags get off on handcuffs and kinky shit, but he can find ways to suggest it."

"Nobody has consensual sex with the kind of bruises I had," Evan said quietly.

Mal inwardly winced, but didn't let it show on his face. "How many people on the jury would know that?"

Evan looked devastated. Mal wanted to take his hand, but Evan had drawn his arms close to his body, shoulders hunched, and Mal had learned his lesson about touching him unexpectedly. So Mal leaned forward and put his hand on the table, palm up, in case Evan wanted to take it.

"Hey," he said, gently. "I'm not saying that I think any of this is true, or that any of this is okay. I'm saying that trials can be unbelievably brutal on victims of sexual assault. I've had people tell me that their rapists' trials were like a second rape, just as bad as the first in a different way. And conviction rates are . . . not great. Juries let off rapists all the time because the defense puts the victim on trial. All the time."

Evan did not touch Mal's hand. Didn't even look at it.

Mal said, "Every day, prosecutors assess their evidence and decide not to proceed, because they think they might not have enough to get a conviction. Maybe the prosecutors in your case weighed the cost—and I don't only mean money—of putting a traumatized juvenile through the ordeal of a trial because they didn't like their odds. Maybe they decided that it would be easier on everyone, including you, to slap the guy in prison for the drug charges, no fuss."

Evan's face was taut with anger. "He got out because he was considered nonviolent. He kidnapped and raped that girl in Reno because of the decisions they made with me."

"Yeah."

"Maybe they thought I was asking for it. Maybe they thought the war on drugs was more important to them than what happened to one tough little methed-up hustler."

"Maybe so," admitted Mal.

Evan dragged his fingertips through the condensation on his beer glass. "So you don't prosecute sexual assaults?"

"I prosecute them all the time," said Mal. "I've got a guy right now who kidnapped and raped his ex, and I'm taking it to trial next week. If I convince the jury, I'll put him away for twenty years, and if I don't, the victim will sit in that courtroom and watch him walk away. Would I have prosecuted Nez? I don't know." He looked at Evan's downturned eyes. "I would have talked to you about the decision, either way. Did they do that?"

"No." Evan sighed. "Oh . . . maybe. I don't know. I wasn't actually in very good shape. Maybe they tried." He rubbed his eyes with the heels of his hands. Then, with some admiration, Mal watched him deliberately relax, drop his arms, and straighten his shoulders, like he was packing up the bad memories and putting them away. He picked up his beer and sipped it. "It was a long time ago."

Mal nodded.

"It's not like I want to spend my life rehashing it," Evan said. "It was a few days. It's not all I ever was or ever will be. But it shouldn't have happened, not to me, not to Emily Trammell. Not to whoever he did it to before me. I hate thinking that it just got erased. Like it doesn't matter."

"It matters," said Mal.

They drank in silence for a minute.

God, Evan was courageous. To move on, after all he'd been through. To keep building a life, even knowing that justice hadn't been done. Mal wished he could make it better for him.

"Evan, did I make you feel like shit? I didn't mean to."

"No," said Evan immediately, a smile in his eyes. "You didn't. Thanks for being so honest, really. I know it's too late to change anything. I appreciate the perspective."

A waitress came and asked them if they wanted another drink; to Mal's surprise, Evan said yes, so he nodded too.

"I think I like this place," said Evan. "I like the music."

The tone of the evening seemed to have just changed. They weren't crime victim and attorney anymore. Now they were two guys drinking and talking about music. Evan met Mal's eyes, biting his lip, and it was like a circuit closing, attraction flowing between them.

Things were looking up.

Smiling, Mal said, "There we disagree." All evening they had been playing a mix of New Wave hits—Dead or Alive, Depeche Mode, Flock of Seagulls. The current selection was "Electric Blue" by Icehouse. Mal knew every single word of this song, and wished he didn't. "This music makes me want to jab knitting needles into my ears."

"Really?" Evan's eyes crinkled. The waitress brought them two glasses of beer. "It's very clubby music, isn't it? Sort of electronic and shallow at worst. No knitting needles required."

"It's like champagne."

"Because it's bubbly?"

"Because I consumed far too much of it in my youth, and now it makes me ill."

Evan gazed at him, a curious light in his eyes, and Mal supposed he owed him a story. "When I was eighteen I got kicked out of my parents' house, so I cashed out my savings account and drove down to Miami, because that seemed like a good place to go be gay. The correct course of action would have been to hit the clubs and sleep with a lot of boys, but instead I hit the clubs and met someone and fell in love. This was *his* music. Twenty-four seven." Reminiscently he said, "One night we snuck up to the rooftop of the Four Seasons, with a CD player and a six-dollar bottle of California sparkly, and danced to New Order in the rain."

"Electric Blue" ended and the thin drum-machine beat of "Blue Monday" commenced. Mal closed his eyes. "Perfect timing," he said. "This *very* song."

"And that's not a pleasant memory?" asked Evan. "Because it sounds awesome."

"It was." *Awesome.* For the first and only time in his life, Mal had willingly become swept up in the storm of someone else's life, and what an exhilarating ascent it had been. Until it stopped, leaving him to plummet to the ground. "But it didn't end so well."

"Sounds like you're not really over it."

"Ah, you know how it is, Doyle," said Mal, raising his beer to his lips. "Some things you learn to live with, whether you're over them or not."

A group bundled into the next booth, talking loudly. Under Mal and Evan's table, the dog got up and shifted around, stepping on Mal's feet.

"Look, do you want to go for a walk or something?" asked Evan unexpectedly. "Dulcie doesn't really like crowded places. She needs to stretch her legs." His eyes crinkled in a smile. "And you need to get out of here before a Duran Duran song makes you cry."

"Good idea. I hate Duran Duran. Lead the way."

They got up and Evan put down money for both of their drinks; Mal let him and followed him and the dog out of the bar, effervescent hope blooming in his chest.

Outside, away from the press of furniture and other people, Dulcie shook herself with a jingle of tags and softly howled at Mal.

"She likes you," said Evan.

"Is there anyone she doesn't like?"

"Not so far," admitted Evan.

The night was clear and had turned cold. In the sky a few stars held their own against the city lights, and the moon shone fitfully between shifting clouds. Evan and Mal let the dog pull them east on Hawthorne, past darkened shops. Music and laughter spilled out of restaurants and bars. Cars hissed past.

"So Dulcie was at Cedar Heights with you today?" asked Mal.

"Yes, they let me bring her," said Evan, his profile momentarily glowing cherry red with a car's reflected taillights. "She helps with my anxiety, and a lot of the residents like her. They don't get to have their own pets there, so they visit with Dulcie. I have to keep her clean, though, and away from the food service areas."

"I have to ask this, Evan, and seriously, I'm not trying to give you crap: don't you find it hard to be in that place every day?"

"No," said Evan, smiling at him. "I'm not— I couldn't be, like, a surgical nurse, or ER. Those people have nerves of steel. But a lot of elder care is about daily maintenance and, you know, just basic kindness. I like taking care of people, and I like old people. They've all got a ton of stories to tell."

"You don't find it a little depressing?" Mal didn't want to bring down the tone of the evening, especially since it seemed to be going so well, but he did wonder how anyone worked in a place like Cedar Heights without wanting to jump out a window.

"The last place I worked was super-depressing," agreed Evan. "All about the bottom line. Some assisted-living companies are publicly traded, so they cut costs and pack people in, to make a buck for the shareholders. Those can be kind of nightmarish. Cedar Heights is nice, though."

"But they *die*."

Mal expected Evan to say something like, *Yes, and they deserve to die with grace and dignity*. Instead he said, "They don't die. They celestially depart."

Mal looked at him incredulously. "They 'celestially depart'?"

"That's right." Evan was smiling a little, his bashful downcast smile. "Or sometimes they enter eternal rest."

Mal began to laugh. "Go on. What else do they do? Are they called home by the Lord Jesus?"

"Not so much in Portland," said Evan. "One of my residents took her last journey to the next universe. A lot of times they just leave this world, which seems nice. Very astronaut-y."

"Let me get this straight, Doyle. The ones who celestially depart, do they go to the same place as the ones who take a journey to the next universe?"

"It's a good question." Evan was still smiling. "I hear that one guy went and returned, but his description of what happened wasn't clear. None of my residents have ever come back to explain."

Mal felt like he was in a pleasant dream, one he couldn't have imagined even a few hours ago. Walking through dark streets under that inconstant moon, shoulder to shoulder with Evan Doyle. Not touching, hands in pockets, but their footsteps matching.

Was it fanciful, to extrapolate from the perfect rhythm of their steps and think about their bodies moving in rhythm in bed? Yes, yes, it was. But every step they took, every step drew them closer. And he was letting Evan pick the route, the destination. With every step, Mal's heart glowed brighter, hope flared hotter.

They had come to a cube of brick-fronted town houses. Mal turned around to walk backward on the sidewalk, facing Evan.

"By the way, this is where I live." Mal looked directly down into Evan's slate-colored eyes. "But you knew that."

CHAPTER EIGHT

Mal was in the spinning center of a galaxy of possibility. It was all down to Evan, whether he would walk through Mal's front door, or walk away.

"Come in, Evan?"

Evan wasn't smiling anymore. His hands were in the pockets of his jacket, his arms tight against his body. Mal gazed into his face, heart beating, waiting for the verdict.

How would they be described, if there were a witness to this moment? Two adult men, standing toe to toe, almost nose to nose. Tense. Poised on the brink of decision.

Did it look like they were about to fight? Or kiss?

Evan said, harshly, "I don't think it would be very smart."

"I think it would be fun."

"I think you're a toppy fucker. I think you're too demanding to accept my limits."

Leaning closer, Mal whispered, "Try me."

Evan hesitated, then exhaled sharply.

"Blowjobs," he said. "Condoms. I go first. And you *do not* touch me with your hands."

Mal widened his eyes. "Oh. Gosh," he said. "Let me think about that for a millisecond. *Okay.*"

He turned, fishing his keys out of his pocket, and ran up the steps to his door. "Come on," he said over his shoulder, snapping the dead bolt open.

To his delight, Evan followed.

Mal intended, upon getting Evan Doyle into his town house, to be a gracious host. He wanted to offer Evan a drink, or a tour, or a towel for Dulcie to lie on. More than anything, he wanted to talk a little, find out where Evan's boundaries were, what things he liked and didn't like. Evan had been through bad shit, and Mal wanted this to be great for him.

But before he had a chance to do more than say, "Would you like—" Evan had grabbed him and was kissing him.

Mal grunted, startled at the hard press of Evan's mouth to his. Evan crowded Mal with his thighs and chest, and he fell gracelessly backward against his living room wall. He caught Evan's waist for balance, and gasped when Evan slapped his hands away, hard enough to sting.

Mal stared at him.

"No hands," said Evan.

"Sorry," said Mal breathily, flattening his palms against the wall. "Right."

Evan clasped Mal's head again, fingers tunneling into his hair, and claimed his mouth. Mal closed his eyes and opened to him, welcoming, but confused. Because Evan was shaking.

"Everything okay?" Mal managed to whisper.

"Shh."

Evan nudged Mal's thighs apart with a knee, so Mal slid down on the wall a little, spreading his legs. Evan accepted the invitation, pressing between his thighs, now the taller; he tugged Mal's head back by the hair and sucked wetly on his throat.

Mal's whole body jolted with excitement. Evan's hands and mouth on him, his lean hips between Mal's thighs—it was a fucking fantasy come true. Except for the fact that he couldn't touch him in return. Except for the nervous tension radiating off Evan.

"Do you—"

"Shut up." Evan backed up the command by kissing him again, licking into his mouth.

Okay. Mal had wanted to talk about what Evan needed, but he was getting the message. Evan apparently needed to be in control.

All yours. Without a word, Mal surrendered. He relaxed his body, let himself go loose and submissive, and grasped his own wrists behind his back.

"Nice," murmured Evan against his mouth. He cupped Mal's jaw and brushed their mouths together softly, his tongue gliding against Mal's, his free hand wandering down his body. The way Evan's touch had gone gentle made Mal's knees turn to water. He moaned into the kiss, blood surging to his groin. Evan's free hand began undressing Mal, stripping off his tie with a yank and unbuttoning the top buttons of his shirt, then stroking over his neck and chest.

Mal hummed with enjoyment and frustration. He didn't love domination games during sex, and he wanted almost more than anything to join in on the groping and stroking. If only he could feel Evan's skin and hair and sweat, smooth his hands over Evan's lovely hard body.

But a deal was a deal. He squeezed his wrists, focused on the sound of their harsh breathing, loud in the quiet room. Evan pressed his hips to Mal's, and Mal moaned at the feel of Evan's dick, hard through their clothes. He was going to suck Evan off, just as soon as he got permission, and the thought made his body flush hot all over, his mouth water with excitement. "Now?" he asked. "Now."

"Lift up your arms."

Mal obeyed and Evan pulled his shirt off. Then Mal returned his hands to the wall while Evan wrenched his own shirt off over his head. Mal got a quick glimpse of Evan's sinewy chest, fuzzy with brown hair, and then Evan was kissing him again. Mal suckled his tongue, wanting more. The curly hair on Evan's chest and belly tickled him, the salty smell of his skin drove him crazy. *More, more.*

Evan broke the kiss, and Malcolm dragged his eyes open.

Let me. He stared into Evan's face. *Tell me to suck you now.*

Evan's fingertips twirled over Mal's nipples, tugging the hair there, sending electric sparks of pleasure through Mal's body. Mal's head fell back against the wall with a thump, mouth open. Now Evan was licking his nipples, and— "Oh my God," Mal whimpered, because that made moisture surge out of him, like a tiny almost-climax, soaking his underwear. The pointed tip of Evan's tongue curled around his nipple again, and then he was dropping to his knees, his mouth hot and wet, on Mal's abs, swirling in his navel, then south. Sucking his skin just above—*so close*—Mal's throbbing cock.

"Evan," managed Mal. "You said. You first."

"That's right," said Evan, now kneeling between Mal's splayed legs, unbuckling his belt with sure hands. "Me first."

Mal bit his lip with anticipation as Evan nuzzled him through the sodden cotton of his briefs. Then his pants and underwear were down around his ankles, and Evan, his lips and breath brushing Mal's shaft, murmured again, "Nice."

There was a crackle of foil, and Mal smelled latex and something sweet. Flavored condom. Appropriately fruity. He gasped as Evan gripped the base of his cock—the heat of Evan's hand lighting him up, the cool latex calming him. He lifted his arms, rested the heels of his hands on the wall above his own head. Oh *yeah*—Evan's mouth closed around his head. Evan sucked pre-come into the reservoir tip of the condom, then licked there, tonguing, squishing slickness and latex against the slit of Mal's cock.

Mal opened his eyes to watch his dick disappear, slowly, into Evan's mouth. *Oh, sweet.*

Evan's eyes were closed, his eyelashes dark crescents on his cheekbones, his face peaceful. Now that he was unquestionably in command, his nervous roughness was gone. His hands and mouth explored Mal's most sensitive places—his balls, his taint, the shaft of his cock—with leisurely enjoyment. Mal trembled, forced himself to relax. He wanted it faster, wanted to come. But more than that, he wanted Evan to have whatever he chose. If Evan preferred to play, he could play.

One of Evan's hands stroked through Mal's pubes and cupped his sack; the other gently and slowly jacked the base of his cock while he sucked, his cheeks hollowed. The condom was a neon lime green, the color shocking against Evan's reddened mouth. Mal loved the sight of that almost as much as he loved the sensation of Evan's tongue as it slid the green around and over his cock's heated skin. He rocked his pelvis in time, wishing he could stroke Evan's hair, tightening his hands into fists to stop himself.

This was *really* good. Evan sucked down the vein on the underside of Mal's cock, turned his head to one side like a flautist to tongue the frenulum, and Mal squeezed his eyes closed against the wave of delight.

Then Evan's incisors scraped Mal's ridge, and the unexpected flash of pain made Mal flinch and whimper. Evan lifted his head just long enough to murmur, "Sorry," and then bent to his task again, lips sheathing the sharp teeth.

"Yes, no problem, thanks," babbled Mal, clinging to the wall for dear life.

Evan started to get serious now, going down hard and deep, mouth and hands working together in a slow and measured rhythm that drove Mal insane.

"Yes, yes, yes." He tried to hold still, to let Evan control him. But he was getting so close, the exquisite tension winding tight in his body. "Yes, oh *God*, you're making me crazy." He pushed back against the wall, arched his spine to push his pelvis forward, his body begging for more, and more, and more.

Abruptly, Evan released him with a squelching *pop* and whispered, "Say please."

Mal couldn't speak. Evan's hand pumped up and down, his lips brushing Mal's glans. "Come on, say please. Beg me."

Mal managed a shuddering whimper.

"Close enough." Evan sucked Mal into his mouth again. Right into the sweltering tightness at the back of his throat. Then he bobbed his head, his hand still fucking the base of Mal's cock, his mouth and tongue and throat taking the rest.

Fiery pressure and need and joy surged up in Mal. Point of no return. He cried out as come pumped out of him in hard prolonged spurts. Mindlessly he tried to thrust his hips, his body seeking more depth. But Evan's big hands held him still as he sucked him through the contractions.

Slowly the tide ebbed, leaving Mal gloriously spent and enervated. He slid down the wall and rested against it, elbows on his knees, hands clasped almost prayerlike before his mouth. Evan's eyes were alight. He grinned at him with a kind of shy pride, his lips shining.

Don't pounce. Don't claim. No hands. *My turn.*

Mal freed himself of the dripping green condom, and then crawled to Evan to press a kiss to his lime-and-latex-tasting mouth.

"Okay if I do that to you?" he whispered.

"Yeah."

"Sit on the couch," Mal suggested, "and take yourself out for me." He wriggled out of the remainder of his clothes while Evan sat on his couch and unzipped his fly. Evan rotated his hips as he pushed his jeans down—and what a fat blunt tool of a dick he had, cut, red, rising up from a curly puff of soft hair. He jacked himself slowly while Mal knee-walked toward him and pulled a bottle of lube and a condom out of the cabinet beside the couch.

Evan's eyebrows went up. Mal smiled at him with anticipation, kneeling in front of the couch between Evan's legs. He unwrapped the condom and dripped lube into it, then handed it to him. "*Voilà.*"

"*Gracias.*" Evan rolled the slippery condom on while Mal, bracing his hands on either side of Evan's hips, watched. He wanted to touch and lick and bite and see Evan everywhere, but they had a deal. Evan had consented to exactly one thing, and he shouldn't press for more, not with this man, not tonight. Evan held the base of his cock, presenting it to him, and Mal leaned forward and drew the head into his mouth. "Yeah, take it all," Evan said, his voice rough with need. It tasted of plain latex, bitter and synthetic. Beneath, Evan's dick was thick and heavy in his mouth, stout and straight. He dragged his tongue over the head, sliding the slickened condom over and around the rigid flesh, then went down until his lips touched Evan's fist.

"God, Mal," Evan said huskily. His free hand cupped Mal's neck, fingers burrowing into his hair. "God, yeah." He let go of his cock and held Mal's head with both hands, his body rippling, pressing up rhythmically into Mal's mouth. Mal tried to slow him down, to gentle him. "Fuck, oh fuck. Oh please," Evan moaned. "Mal, don't tease me, don't, I can't—"

"You teased me," murmured Mal, nuzzling the trail of wiry hair on Evan's abdomen.

"I just— Just please— I need it."

Mal hummed with assent and swallowed him down as deep as he could go, sucked him hard. "Oh yes, oh fuck, oh God, that's it," chanted Evan, while Mal nodded his head in a hard, steady rhythm, sucking Evan's latex-covered cock into his throat, pulling back, sucking in. Evan's body arched, his hips pulsed. Grasping Mal's head, he began to fuck his mouth, urgently and without finesse. "Make me come. Need it. Yeah."

Mal tightened his grip on the couch cushions and willingly took it, all of it, his jaw and throat muscles relaxed, tears forming from the effort. Evan undulated, needy, dirty words spilling out of his mouth with each stroke. "Fuck. Fuck. Yes. I'm almost. Fuck. Mal." He slapped his palm on the couch. "*Fuck*!"

Mal opened his tear-blurred eyes and watched Evan come: lips parted, eyes closed, tendons of his throat taut.

Beautiful.

Mal sprawled, unselfconsciously naked, on the couch, while Evan gathered up his clothes. He watched with appreciation while Evan turned his back and zipped up his jeans.

That was a world-class ass. Mal himself was a man of very little ass, and he drowsily rested his head in his folded arms and allowed his gaze to linger.

Maybe someday he'd get lucky enough to be allowed to touch that ass. There was so much more he wanted to do.

Evan, shoes in hands, bent over slightly to examine a small framed snapshot on the wall. Mal was sadly aware that he had not inherited the gay man's supposed knack for interior decorating: his town house was tasteful enough, but sparse. He had no art on his walls—except for that picture.

Evan glanced at Mal over his shoulder. "Is that you on the right?"

"Uh-huh."

He turned back and studied the picture, smiling. "I would not have guessed that you were ever into drag."

"I think it's obvious that I wasn't very good at it," said Mal. "*He* was into it, and I was into him."

"This is Miami?"

"Yep."

Evan was putting on his shoes now. He was going to walk away from this like it was a one-time hookup. A little impersonal exchange of spit and come between acquaintances. Like he hadn't demanded that Mal beg for release, like he hadn't begged for it himself.

"I need it. I'm almost. Yes."

Evan shrugged into his jacket. Dulcie was on her feet, wagging her yellow tail. She'd been politely curled up on Mal's kitchen rug, apparently undisturbed by the spectacle of her master getting his genitals sucked by a near-stranger. Now she stood expectantly by the door.

Ready to go home.

Mal said casually, "Do this again sometime?"

Evan gave him a quick smile from under his eyelashes, patting his pockets for his keys and phone. Not making any promises.

Mal had willingly accepted a passive role during sex. Now he was forced into an equally passive role: the needy one. The one who wanted more. He didn't enjoy it as much.

Evan wasn't going to call. They weren't even friends.

"With regular treatments, Doyle," he said coldly, "maybe you'll last longer than thirty seconds."

The smile congealed on Evan's face. His nostrils flared.

"Night, Umbertini," he said coolly, and left. The door shut behind him, not with a slam, but a decisive *click*.

"Damn," sighed Mal.

CHAPTER NINE

The following day, Friday, was the first day of Evan's weekend. He was cutting drywall for his bedroom. It was fiddly, exacting work—the room was an erratic gabled space tucked under the vault of the roof, all odd angles and nonparallel lines—and he kept making mistakes.

His head ached from too little sleep. Last night had been bad, in spite of the outstanding sex with Mal. His old familiar problems: hyperalertness, free-form anxiety, the uncontrolled rush of adrenaline as though he faced some immediate threat. Insomnia. To calm his nerves, he'd brushed Dulcie until she shone like brass, keeping her up well past her bedtime. When he finally slept it had been restless, interrupted by black dreams and nervy bouts of wakefulness.

"Woooo!" cried Dulcie from the downstairs laundry room, where he'd locked her to keep her out of the drywall dust.

He glanced out the window to see Caroline's car in the driveway. Tossing his measuring tape aside, he went downstairs to let her in.

"Did anyone follow you up here?" he asked, as he opened the door and she stepped inside. She was dressed nice, in a little skirt and boots, and when she opened her arms to him he backed away. "Don't, I'm covered in gypsum. It's gross."

"Okay." She handed him her jacket, and he hung it up. "No, no one followed me up here. Why would they?"

"I dunno. Just having the kind of day where that seems like a reasonable concern."

"Yeah? You have days like that a lot?"

"It's not too rare."

He ushered her into the kitchen, and she perched on a kitchen stool. Dulcie's piteous whimpers were audible even through the closed laundry room door, and she said, "Your dog is in some kind of distress."

"I'll get her. Hang on, I'm gonna go change my shirt too."

He released Dulcie from the laundry room, stripped out of his shirt in a cloud of noxious dust, and washed his hands and face in the laundry room sink. "Calm down," he said to his reflection in the mirror.

Tugging on a clean shirt from the dryer, he headed back to the kitchen, where he found Dulcie half in Caro's lap. He laughed. "You can push her down."

"I love her," said Caro, her hands buried in Dulcie's soft yellow ruff. "What's gypsum?"

He poured them glasses of cold water, and they sat together in the kitchen while he told her about the drywall project. DIY home repair had apparently not been part of her education, but she grasped his problem immediately: "You always did suck at geometry."

"Yep."

"I could help."

"I'm actually almost done. Have you ever painted? You can help me paint, when I'm ready."

"It doesn't look hard on TV."

"It isn't." He smiled at her. "That would be great."

"Sooo." She swirled the water around in her glass. "Last night you met Mal for a beer?"

"Did he tell you that?"

"He texted me right before. Go on?"

What could he say? The memory of Mal, pleasured and moaning, came into his mind. Malcolm with his pants around his ankles and his cute narrow little butt clenching in Evan's hands, his long, slim dick in Evan's mouth.

Evan should have just dropped to his knees and brought him off fast. Should have kept it impersonal. Instead he had yielded to temptation: kissed him, and explored him. The smell of chlorine had risen from Mal's warmed skin, like he'd gone for a swim that day. And he had a swimmer's body, with lean lithe muscles and silky straight body hair.

Evan had expected a bossy and demanding Mal, but he'd gotten exactly the opposite: a compliant Mal, who had given him exactly what he wanted and nothing, not one thing, that he didn't. Unselfish Mal, sprawled naked and beautiful on his couch, long-limbed and languorous.

Then without warning, Mal had taunted him. Dark eyes shining with mockery.

Asshole.

To Caroline he said, "I ran into him at Cedar Heights when he was visiting his mom. I'd been wanting to ask him some questions about what happened to me. About, you know, some of the decisions the prosecutors made. So I asked Mal."

"Why didn't you ask me?"

"I wanted to. I want to talk to you about it." He ran a hand through his hair. "But, Kiki, to be honest, some of the stuff that happened to me was pretty gross, and I don't want you to think of me like that."

"About Nez? It was like what happened to her?"

"Yeah."

She put her feet up on the chair, folded her arms over her knees. "I could never think any less of you. You know that."

"I know. I do. I— It tore me up when you cried, though. I just—I don't want to have secrets from you, but I don't want to make you cry, either."

She paused. "I get that, Boxy. I have stuff I haven't told you too."

"Bad stuff?"

"Stuff that orphans do," she said, lifting one shoulder. "I haven't always been very smart. But I don't want you to take responsibility for things that weren't your fault."

It was all *my fault,* whispered an insidious voice in his mind. He shook his head: she was telling him that it wasn't. She didn't need his crazy.

"Fair enough," he said. "I'll try not to. I want to know everything."

"I do too."

"Then we'll talk," he said. "We'll talk. We have time, Kiki. I'm not going anywhere."

"Promise?"

"I promise."

"Okay," she said softly. "So. Did Mal give you what you were looking for?"

Oh, and more. So funny, the way just the mention of his name made Evan's skin flush all over, like a wash of heat. Little hairs at the base of his spine prickled and stood up.

"I can't figure him out," he said. "He seems so arrogant and dickish, but actually he was pretty helpful." And unexpectedly vulnerable sometimes, and weirdly sweet. Until the arrogant dickish armor came back up.

"And did you thank him by snogging him?"

Evan hesitated. "What does *he* say?"

Caroline laughed, a long and delighted peal. "You did! You did! You snogged Mal!"

Heat bloomed in Evan's face. "What did he say?"

"Nothing, I haven't talked to him. Come on, tell."

"Kiki—"

"Tell, tell, tell," she sang.

"Ugh, this sucks. Can we go back to the part of our lives where you thought I was dead? Because that might have been the right choice."

"I am shocked, *shocked* by your use of dark humor," said Caroline. "But not distracted. Nope. Tell me everything."

Yeah, right. He pushed aside the memory of Mal swallowing his dick like he'd never even heard of a gag reflex. "It was no big deal."

"Boxy, Mal doesn't do casual."

"Uh-huh," said Evan. "I might know a different side of him than you do."

"Really?" Far from being dissuaded, Caroline sounded intrigued. "Is he a good kisser?"

Indeed he was. And his body was golden-skinned and hard. Sensitive nipples, a tongue like hot velvet, and the noises he made as he approached orgasm were soft and appreciative and dangerously thrilling. "Not discussing."

"Did you do more than kiss?"

"Sure," said Evan, laughing a little. "He insulted me like a kid on the schoolyard."

"What'd you do to piss him off?"

Evan crossed his arms. "Why do you assume that it was something I did?"

"No fault, Boxy, but Mal digs you," said Caroline. "He wants to buy you a corsage and take you to prom."

"Uh-huh."

"I'm serious. You've seen it yourself. The arrogant dickish thing is a front. Mal throws his heart into things. I'm not just talking about relationships, but everything. He's a serious guy. He doesn't fuck around."

"Again," said Evan, "I think I know a different side of him than you do."

A pause. What had he just said? Evan squeezed his eyes shut with dismay.

Caroline said, "*Alex*. Did you have sex with Mal Umbertini?"

Don't call me that. He just managed to not hiss it aloud. Taking a steadying sip of water, he said, "Wow, you know what? I have a lot to do today. Maybe you should go."

"Alex. Evan. Box."

"Caro." She'd acquired the nickname in college; he'd never called her that before. "This is not a thing, with me and Mal."

"But is it a thing with Mal and you?"

He rubbed his forehead. "What?"

"When I call him, what's he going to tell me?"

"Nothing."

Actually, that was probably true. Mal was obnoxious and arrogant, but Evan believed he'd maintain confidentiality.

But he could be wrong.

"Ask him and see, I guess," he said, sighing. "You've known him a long time. But, Kiki, I don't know what you're picturing here. I used to give blowjobs for money." Wow, it was hard to say that out loud. His face went hot and his eyes stung. "Mal might be a guy who does serious, but he's not going to do serious with *me*."

She considered him, her head tilted. "Do you think Mal doesn't have a past? He does. Not the same as yours, but bad enough that he's not going to be fazed by what you did when you were a minor."

"He doesn't know everything." He paused. "You don't know everything."

"I know I don't." Her voice was soft.

He needed to tell her. She deserved to know. She had to have guessed part of it; it wasn't right to not give her the truth about what happened to their mother, to Derrick, just because it was hard for him.

"I told you . . . being in the En wasn't so bad. I mean, it wasn't fun, but I knew what to do, and no one had asked me for more than I was willing to do. Until Derrick brought Nez on Thanksgiving. And then . . . it went sideways so fast, Kiki. Nez was not satisfied with my little schoolboy blowjobs, and when I refused it . . . he got violent between one second and the next. I can't— I couldn't even tell the story in order for a long time. Some of it's still a blur."

But some details were still terrible, crisp and clear in his memory.

"Please tell me," whispered Caroline.

He nodded.

"Nez tried to . . . He tried to pin me down and strip off my pants. He was bigger than me and I was scared. Struggling. Derrick jumped in and tried to help hold me down. Mom—Mom had never really— she was sort of out of it most of the time and she'd never really tried to step in before. But I was struggling with Derrick and Nez, and yelling, and she woke up and started screaming. She jumped on Derrick and was yelling at him to let me go."

"What happened?" she whispered.

"Derrick threw her off him. He threw her down, and her head hit the corner of that little table. Remember, the one with the leaves in the top? And she was dead. I don't think he actually meant to . . . Anyway." He kept his eyes on his glass of water. "I freaked out, and it's kind of a blur, but I threw Derrick out the window."

There was an awful pause. So quiet that Evan could hear the branches of a tree, creaking against one of the upstairs windows. He'd have to prune that back away from the house.

"You what?" asked Caroline.

"I picked up Derrick like a doll, and threw him out the window."

She drank some water. "They said—I always thought—that the third person in the En had killed Mom and Derrick, and that you saw it and ran away."

"I was the third person," said Evan. "Derrick killed Mom. I killed Derrick. And Nez, the fourth person, bashed me on the head and put me in his truck, and drove away."

She was silent for a long moment.

"You're not surprised, right?" he said, laughing nervously. "I told you it wasn't Nez, and no one else was there. So."

"I shouldn't be, I guess." Her voice was quiet. "But . . . Oh, Alex."

"I'm sorry." Sweat was beading on his face, and his lungs felt tight. "I'm sorry, Caroline. I should have— I think about what I should have done, I wish I had, but it all happened so fast, and I couldn't—"

She got up and came to him and put her forehead on his shoulder, not really hugging him, not crying. He braced his feet, supporting her weight.

"I'm sorry," he whispered again.

"*I'm* sorry." She wrapped her arms around him and squeezed tight. "It's not our fault, though. Not mine, and not yours. Someone should have protected us. I don't remember feeling like a child, but we were children. We should have been safe."

"Yeah." Her hair smelled good, like some expensive shampoo, but under that she smelled just like she always had, like his family. "Mom . . . she did try. I'm not saying it wasn't too little, too late, but she died trying, Kiki."

Caroline nodded. He knew she had her own knotty relationship with her memories, one Evan couldn't untangle for her. "Anyway," he went on, "when they arrested me, I told them all about it. I thought they'd put me in prison. I didn't care, I just . . . But they didn't. Didn't do anything about it at all."

"It's still on the books as an unsolved case."

"I don't know why. I always thought . . . maybe the reason they didn't prosecute me for manslaughter, at least, was because they knew what Nez did to me, and they thought that was, like, punishment enough for what I'd done—"

She lifted her head. "That is *not* how prosecutors are supposed to work."

"No, well. Mal explained some things that I hadn't thought of before. So, yeah. Maybe that's not what happened. But still. Maybe to them she was just some junkie whore, and the guy who killed her was dead, and it was too much paperwork to bother with? I don't know."

"I'll look into it."

"You don't have to."

"Yes, I do."

Yeah. She undoubtedly did.

They stood like that for a minute, and then she stepped away, wiped her eyes. "I'm glad you told me. Are you okay?"

"Sure," he said shakily, "unless you start rattling cages and get me arrested for murdering Derrick."

"Trust me," she said.

"Yeah. I do."

But she could probably tell that recalling these old memories was taking a toll on his sense of peace. Unresolved tension crawled along his nerves. He would abandon the drywall project for the day, go for a long hike with Dulcie. Exercise and solitude were still the best anxiety treatments that he knew. "Are you okay?"

"I will be. I guess I'd better let you get back to work." She forced a bright smile. "Hey, meet me for lunch sometime this week?"

He hesitated.

Anxiety told him not to be seen with her in public. They looked too much alike. If someone wanted to find him, they'd watch her.

"I don't know—"

"Come on. Tomorrow at noon, we'll meet in a café somewhere downtown. It'll be crowded at lunchtime. No one will even notice."

"Caroline." His patience had worn thin. "Stop pushing."

"Okay, but we—"

"You push. You always have. But I need you to listen to me now when I tell you to stop pushing."

"Okay." She ran a hand through her hair. "You're right."

"I'm not going anywhere, okay? You don't have to keep pushing me."

"I know," she said, contritely. "I'm sorry. I'm not pushing. But I'm asking. Want to do lunch sometime? Whenever works for you."

He sighed. It would be nice. But just now, he couldn't decide—couldn't tell—if it was a bad idea or not, to do something normal with his sister like buy her lunch. "Text me the time and place. I'll try."

"I will. And I'm going to interrogate Mal too, don't think I won't."

He rolled his eyes. "See you later, Caroline."

"Bye, Box."

He was still feeling unsettled the next week, heading into downtown Portland to meet Caroline for lunch. Parking was terrible. He and Dulcie walked several blocks toward the vegan diner where, she'd said, the roasted Portobello burgers were to die for.

It was as he approached the diner that he began to get scared.

Chills up the back of his neck. His scalp prickling, the hairs standing up on his arms. Like someone was following him. Like someone was watching.

He halted in the middle of the sidewalk.

This was *stupid*. No one was looking for Alex Farkas. No one was stalking Caroline Farkas in order to get to him. There were no organized crime figures, no Nez, hiding behind mushroom sandwiches, ready to strike.

But as he'd said to Mal and Caroline on the phone, it didn't work that way. Just because there wasn't anything to be anxious about didn't mean he wasn't anxious. In the same way that it raked his soul to tell her that he used to give blowjobs for money, even though she already knew.

He felt defenseless and exposed, like even the cloudy sky was watching him. Dulcie's head was up, ears alert and tail low as she glanced around her. She didn't seem worried, though. She seemed to have picked up on his alarm, and was trying to locate its source. After a moment she turned and stared at him over her shoulder, with a puzzled air.

He was an *idiot*.

Clicking his tongue to Dulcie, he turned left randomly, and walked a few blocks, hoping that the prickling on the back of his neck would pass.

He kept walking, not really watching where he was going, focused on the itch between his shoulder blades. Fleeing from nothing, dogged by fears that he knew were irrational. It didn't matter. He just couldn't go to that café.

He texted his sister: *Sorry. I'm too freaked out. Try again next week?*

They were walking past a square park with a bronze statue of a soldier in it when he saw Mal. He was cutting through the park toward a gray building, dressed in a suit and a black wool overcoat, briefcase in hand. And seeing him there seemed to make everything all right. Maybe it was because he had told Mal so much, and received no judgment, but the sight of him made everything that felt out of true click into place.

"Mal," he called impulsively.

Mal turned and his eyes widened. Evan, suddenly hyperaware of how loud his voice had been, glanced around. They were right in front of the Multnomah County Courthouse, where both Mal and Caro worked. The people around him on these sidewalks and in this park were wearing suits. Lawyers—Mal's colleagues, presumably—all over the place.

Damn.

Mal glanced at his watch as he came toward Evan. "Doyle. Is everything okay?"

"Yeah. I mean, no," Evan said. "I'm being a total neurotic. Anyway, I—I saw you, and I thought— Mal, can I buy you lunch?"

Malcolm blinked. Evan blushed, feeling like an idiot.

Mal wanted casual sex, not a relationship. Not to be stalked on his lunch hour, where his colleagues could see, by *Evan*.

But Mal said, "I'd love to." He looked at his watch again. "Unfortunately, in eight minutes a judge is going to grant a motion to dismiss one of my cases, and I need to be there."

Evan noticed, belatedly, that Mal looked a little tired. A little tense. Troubled, actually. "I'm sorry. I'm a dumbass. I'd better go."

"You're not a dumbass. I'm just in the middle of a shitty day." Mal smiled, that single dimple appearing in one cheek. "Hey. Rain check?"

"Sure."

"Give me a kiss to seal the deal."

"What? No."

"Why not?"

Why not? Evan shifted his feet, glancing around nervously. "You work with these people."

"And they will be so jealous." Mal's voice had gone low and purring, just like it had been the other night when he'd said, *"Try me."* That irresistible dare. "Lay it on me. I'll be the envy of every woman here, and approximately three to ten percent of the men. Depending on which survey you read."

"Do they teach this in law school?" demanded Evan. "You and Caroline both. You *push*."

Mal's smile faltered; his eyebrows crooked. "No." Evan saw him remember who he was talking to: the victim, the boy with the zip ties. "I'm—"

God, Mal Umbertini. Sometimes you just had to kiss him to shut him up.

Evan fisted his lapels and kissed him firmly. *Not a victim.* Mal kept his arms at his sides and didn't move, so Evan broke the kiss. Before he could pull away, Mal tilted his head and leaned in, and his lips covered Evan's sweetly. Evan's *shut up* turned into *Hello, hi, I'm happy to see you.* Mal's tongue brushed Evan's lower lip and then he sucked on it.

Evan sighed with pleasure and opened his mouth, just touching the tip of his tongue to Mal's. His blood heated and his cock tingled. He wanted to melt against Mal's body.

God, what was he doing? They were in public. He let Mal go.

Mal's dark eyes were half-closed, shadowed by his lashes. "Thank you, Evan."

"You're welcome."

Mal smiled his crooked little smile. "It's funny, kissing without moving my hands. Do I look like I'm being molested?"

"No, you just look like a bottom."

Mal laughed with real amusement, throwing his head back, and Evan laughed with him, light-headed. He bounced on his heels, trying to get his semi to go down.

Then Mal glanced at his watch again, and his smile dimmed. "Ah, well. This is definitely the pleasantest thing that's going to happen to me today, but now I have to go get kicked in the teeth."

"Oh. Okay." Sobered by the clouds in Mal's eyes, Evan added, "Um, are you okay?"

"I've had better days. See you around?"

"Yeah."

Mal started to walk away, then turned on his heel and strode back to where Evan was still standing. "Listen—" He hesitated.

"What?"

"Come over after work. To my place. Please."

Oh, he shouldn't. That had been a one-time thing. But he wanted to. He'd been longing for a way back to Mal's town house ever since he'd left it. And he wanted to alleviate that dejected expression in Mal's eyes. Evan was a sucker for people who seemed to need help.

"It'll be kind of late. After nine."

The crooked smile reappeared—wry and a little smug. "Oh, I'll be up."

Reclining bonelessly on Mal's couch later that night, his body glowing with the aftermath of orgasm, Evan stroked Mal's hair. It was short and thick and straight, plush against his palm, like a cat's fur. Mal was sitting on the floor, back against the couch, not touching Evan, but allowing himself to be caressed.

Rain drummed on the roof of Mal's town house. Rain rolled down the windows, making the streetlight that shone on Mal's skin waver and blur. The dark room smelled like sex and sweat and flavored condoms.

Evan had been incredibly nervous when he'd come here after work. He'd brought a box of his favorite condoms, like a bouquet of flowers. But Mal had seemed so happy to see him, and he had given himself to Evan like a gift, so trustingly, so gladly. It was gorgeous, how that trust made him feel.

He now dragged the backs of his fingers over Mal's sandpapery jaw. Mal turned his head and kissed the heel of Evan's hand, just above his leather bracelet. Then he gently bit him, and glanced up at Evan through dark eyelashes. "Is that okay?" he mumbled against Evan's skin.

"Uh-huh." He brushed his thumb over Mal's lips. "I like the way you go all nonverbal when you're turned on."

"Glad you like it, because I can't help it. The talking part of my brain just shuts off."

"I wouldn't have thought the talking part of your brain ever shut off," Evan laughed. "It's your superpower, and sex is your kryptonite."

Mal huffed with amusement. "I was once with a guy who loved dirty talk, and I totally couldn't do it. I wanted to, but all I could do was grunt like an animal."

"It's cute."

Evan could feel Mal smile against his palm. "You've got the dirty talk."

"I'm not sure saying 'fuck' over and over really counts as dirty talk."

"It's very clear," said Mal. "Excellent communication skills."

"Thanks, I'll update my résumé."

Mal nuzzled an openmouthed kiss to Evan's inner forearm. Evan's skin jumped; he hadn't known he was so sensitive there.

"I didn't tell Caroline anything," he said, "about us."

"Same here," said Mal, his voice slightly muffled by Evan's skin. "But that doesn't mean she doesn't know. The act of not answering her questions probably serves as confirmation. Of something."

His tongue flickered out to lick the hollow inside of Evan's elbow, tasting him. Evan shivered; it was like he could feel the brush of that tongue all the way up his spine. He tucked the feeling away in his memory, to recall later.

Mal said casually, "So what do you do for sex?"

"You know exactly what I do."

Mal smiled. "No, I mean . . . Grindr? OKCupid? I don't see you picking up boys at CC Slaughters."

"No," agreed Evan, a little wistfully. "When I lived in San Diego I would hook up sometimes. I met people when I was in nursing school, or other nurses, or whatever."

"You had fuck buddies," said Mal. "No steady boyfriend?"

"No. I had a girlfriend for a while, but it didn't work out."

"A girl . . . friend?" he asked, like it was an alien concept.

"Uh-huh. That was a long time ago."

"And you don't have fuck buddies up here?"

There was a guy living on a boat who was good for an undemanding mutual suck-off once in a while, but he was frequently drunk and always hard to reach. Another guy, married and cheating on his wife, who made Evan feel like shit. His one dating-service hookup had ended catastrophically when the guy had grabbed Evan in his excitement and tried to get rough with him.

"Good fuck buddies aren't easy to find," he admitted. "What do you do?"

"I date," said Mal with a shrug.

"You date?"

"You know. Coffee, drinks, dinner and a movie. Sex on the third date, if you like each other. Or even if you don't sometimes."

"But always it's, like, a relationship?"

He shrugged again, smiling ruefully. "That's the idea. The last several attempts have not exactly worked out." His eyes glowed in the dimness. "And then there's you."

"We're not dating," said Evan flatly.

"No. I'm your latest fuck buddy."

Evan snorted. "You're nobody's fuck buddy, Mal."

Mal pretended to be affronted. "I could be a fuck buddy."

Evan slid down on the couch, bringing his face closer to Mal's. "Listen," he said, meeting Mal's eyes. "This is all I do. I'm not going to get used to you, like a woodland creature eating an apple out of your hand or whatever." Mal's smile broadened, his eyes bright with laughter. Okay, that wasn't a very sexy metaphor. But Evan persisted, "We're not going to fuck. Ever. The hands thing . . . it's a hard line. I can't cross it."

"Or what?"

"I'm not going to cross it," clarified Evan.

The truth he couldn't admit was that he was terrified of having a full-blown panic attack during sex. An event so humiliating, so paralyzing, it might create its own triggers, like a forest fire creating its own weather. Make it impossible for him to enjoy sex at all.

He'd come a long way, to be able to give and take as much as he did. That one little sexual activity that he could do, to help him feel connected to another man once in a while. He couldn't bear to lose it.

But Mal was right about one thing—he wanted a lot more than he was currently getting.

He hated living in fear. Fear of fear, panic induced by panic. Fear that changed his behavior and his life, made him veer to avoid anything that might set off his panic.

How could he hope to explain to someone like Mal, who was so fearless, how an old memory—*a hand on his skin, hard and powerful, wrapped around his cock*—was enough to make him nauseous with dread? Mal was confident enough to cede control; Evan was living his life in fear of a man who wasn't even there.

"Okay," said Mal, who'd been watching him thoughtfully. "I won't cross it either. Offer still stands. No dates, no strings. Call me when you want to get off."

"Why?" asked Evan, genuinely bewildered. "I— Kiki told you about Derrick? About the En?"

"Yeah."

"So you know. I'm— I'm not—"

"It's fun for now." Mal's voice was casual. "It's fun, Evan. That's all. I like what you do with your tongue."

"Are you telling me you wouldn't rather be with someone a little less screwed up? Because I don't believe you."

"Are you turning me down for my own good?" countered Mal. "Because *boring*."

Evan smiled at him shyly. "I'm not turning you down at all," he admitted. "I can't stay away. I just don't get it."

In answer, Mal leaned up and kissed him.

His kiss was pure lazy dirty sex, sinuous tongue and banked aggression, a deep demanding exploration that melted Evan's resistance and nearly set him on fire. He'd been about to get up and find his clothes—he didn't do overnighters, obviously—but now he was falling into Mal with a kind of helpless desperation, tasting used watermelon condom and Mal's hunger. Mal was rising up off the floor and getting onto the couch, not pinning Evan but kneeling upright, making Evan arch up to keep kissing him.

Mal pressed a condom into his hand and Evan fumbled to get it onto his alert dick. Nuzzling kisses to his hips and thighs, Mal settled between his legs. *What am I doing?* Evan never did this. Never went first. He liked to bleed off his partner's tension, take his pleasure at the end when he was more relaxed.

Although they were both pretty relaxed from before.

Mal's wicked mouth closed over the head of Evan's cock, his tongue imperiously palpating the ridge. "Oh shit," moaned Evan, collapsing back onto the couch. "I can't believe this."

Mal sucked him, then released him with an obscene *smack*. "I don't get what you don't get," he said huskily. "How am I supposed to resist this cock?"

Evan's eyes closed while Mal drew him right into his throat, engulfing him with a slow, controlled suction that made his hips rise up off the cushions. Evan liked to suck cock—he was good at it, and he enjoyed the power and control it gave him—but it seemed to really turn Mal's crank.

"You love that," growled Evan, and Mal made a wordless hum that clearly translated to *Hell yes*.

Evan grasped the thick base of his dick, the few inches that Mal couldn't take in, and they moved together, Mal's tongue doing lascivious things to Evan's head while Evan's hand ran up and down his shaft.

"Fuck, that's good," Evan mumbled, free hand grasping Mal's hair. "Oh God. Mal. Oh fuck. Why do I—let you. Oh, *fuck*."

He turned his face into the back of the couch and, for an exquisite moment, he allowed himself to imagine what he really wanted: Mal on top of him, Mal's beautiful cock inside him, Mal driving into him with hard thrusts of his hips. The fantasy felt almost-true as orgasm swept over him, raced through and surged out of him. Mal groaned and the vibration made Evan shudder, suddenly oversensitive.

Mal drew off, mouth wet, eyes black and huge.

There, in the crazy endorphin-rush of sex, Evan thought he could do it. He could roll over right now, and offer himself up to Mal. Right now. Mal would be kind. Mal wouldn't hurt him.

But, no. He couldn't. He *couldn't*.

Evan slid off the couch and knelt before Mal. *This is enough*, he assured himself. *This is good too.*

Later, Evan fumbled for his clothes in the dark. Mal was sprawled on the couch, eyes closed. He might be asleep. Hoping to flee from Mal's town house without any more conversation, Evan quietly pulled on his pants.

Intimate, that's how it felt. Good, yes, but uncomfortably intimate, like they were learning things about each other, private things. There was raw emotional vulnerability in Mal's eyes during sex. Evan wasn't sure what that meant, but it wasn't the marshmallow fluff that Caroline thought was inside Mal. Mal was boiling with something that he didn't show everyone, a molten core of passion that both attracted Evan and frightened him.

What he really wanted was to be close to Mal, to know more about his secrets, to please him and bask in his attention. He shook his head as he buckled his belt and searched for his shoes.

Just *fun for now*, hah. Mal's "fun for now" might wreck him.

He was putting on his jacket when Mal rolled off the couch and to his feet. Evan watched as he padded to the kitchen and rummaged in a drawer.

"Here." He offered Evan a little scrap of bronze metal.

Evan took it. "Mal," he said, "fuck buddies do not give each other keys."

"Maybe you can't sleep some night," Mal said. "It's 2 a.m., you're horny. Think of me."

A grin pulled on Evan's lips. "I'm sure I will."

Mal grinned back. "And come over."

"At 2 a.m.? What if you have a date?"

Mal shrugged. "Maybe call first. I'll try to work you in."

Smiling, Evan clipped the key onto his own ring. He doubted he'd ever use the key, but he was touched nonetheless. "Thanks."

CHAPTER TEN

Be there in about 30 minutes.

"Yes," said Mal, softly, and tossed his phone onto the bed. "Yes, yes, yes."

The text was from Evan, in response to Mal's *Come over?* It was the twelfth time he'd invited Evan over in the last two weeks. Only the eighth time Evan had agreed to come.

Mal tunelessly sang "It's a Wonderful Night" to himself as he stripped out of his clothes. Evan got off work at nine, and it was only 8:50, so he had a little time. Heart beating fast, he took a hot shower, thoroughly cleaning but otherwise ignoring his dick, which was all excited. It didn't need much more foreplay than this: the chime of a text from Evan Doyle. Yes, yes, yes.

He put on pajama bottoms and danced, shirtless, around the town house, picking up clutter and making sure everything was ready. It was acceptably clean. There was beer in the refrigerator— IPA, the same kind Evan had ordered that day they'd met at Pettygrove's bar. Snacks too, in case Evan decided to stay and eat. He never had before. There were also condoms in the table beside the couch. Condoms upstairs in his bedroom too, and fresh sheets on the bed. Not that Evan had ever come upstairs, either.

But you never knew. It could happen.

Nine fifteen. It was full dark outside, threatening rain. Mal dimmed the lights in the living room, then turned them off and turned on a table lamp, instead. That was better. Or maybe he should light candles, instead? No, candles would be trying too hard. The lamp made it look cozy and shadowy, but not deliberately seductive.

Stop dithering, Zach would say. *Own the room.*

It was undignified and embarrassing, this rush of eager joy, because Evan was coming over tonight. But Mal couldn't help it. He was so into him. It wasn't just the sex—not that he didn't love the sex, but he'd had plenty of sex. It was Evan.

His heart had leapt like a deer, two weeks ago, when Evan had called his name in front of the courthouse. That had been the second time Evan had sought him out, and it had clearly been difficult for him to do so. Evan had been nervous, but had approached. Evan had been exasperated, but had kissed him. Mal had made some joke, but under his humor he'd been astonished and moved. That had been when he fully realized his own feelings: he was in deep.

Evan was smart and funny and brave. He had a kind and generous spirit, locked inside prickly hedgehog armor. He was hot as hell. And he was . . . He was Mal's man, and Mal was his. Somehow his heart had settled upon this man—this one—and he couldn't imagine wanting anyone else this way, ever.

It was like the rush of devotion he'd once felt for Zach. But not like it too, because he was grown now. Though technically an adult at eighteen, he'd been too immature to really understand what he'd wanted from Zach—not just a lover but a guide, a replacement for his lost family. Someone to tell him who he was and how to get on in the world.

Now, he knew who he was and what he wanted. He could keep an eye on the long-term goal while taking care of the short-term details. And short-term: he wanted Evan to feel safe and welcome here. For him to like being here, with Mal.

He was reconsidering the candle question when he heard Evan's footsteps, the jingle of Dulcie's dog tags, on the stoop outside. Controlling his urge to throw open the door, he waited for the doorbell. It didn't ring.

Evan was hesitating.

Don't push. Let him come. Mal mentally began to recite the Gettysburg Address.

Finally, after a long moment, Evan rang the doorbell.

"We can not dedicate, we can not consecrate, we can not hallow this ground." Mal walked calmly to the door and opened it.

Evan's shoulders were tense, his jaw set. He stepped through the doorway and immediately looked down and away, bracing himself against one wall as he toed off his shoes.

How could Mal tell him that he had nothing, nothing to be nervous about? Mal only knew one way. He said nothing, closed the door behind him, and bent to greet Dulcie, who danced around his knees and woofed at him, while Evan shucked his jacket. He petted the dog's silky ears. *At least someone's happy to see me.*

With any other guest in the world, he'd offer to take their jacket, get them something to drink. Perform the usual rituals of welcome. But he'd learned, over eight visits, that Evan did not always like those rituals. Sometimes, when he was feeling anxious or guarded—like tonight—they made him more uncomfortable, not less. Evan was here for sex, not conversation or friendship or affection, and he didn't like it when the lines blurred. Not until after, anyway.

So Mal waited until Evan looked at him, and then he lifted his arms, laced his fingers behind his head.

Evan's eyes flared. Without a word, he stepped up to Mal and touched him, hands cool and callused on Mal's sides. Mal bent his legs to fit himself against Evan, and hummed with pleasure as Evan ran his hands up and down Mal's back. *Yes, whatever you like.* Evan felt strong; he smelled so good, a little sweaty. Mal dared to taste the humid skin of Evan's neck. And then Evan was kissing him, with chapped lips and urgency, and Mal tipped his head and opened his mouth to Evan's sweeping tongue. Unthinkingly, he lifted a leg to draw Evan's hips closer, to get a little friction on his erection. Evan caught the back of his knee and pulled him up to ride his thigh.

Yeah.

Mal kept his hands behind his head and melted against Evan, trusting Evan to hold him upright as they ground against each other. Even drowning in delight, he still had just enough brain capacity to marvel—Evan was *here*, Evan came to Mal for this, and oh *damn*, he was awed and stupid with joy. There was so much more he wanted, so much about this arrangement that was unsatisfying, but in this moment, none of that mattered: Evan was here, and nothing had ever been better.

Evan walked him backward into the living room and put him in an armchair, then knelt between his knees to pull off his pajama pants. Mal obediently lifted his hips, his fingers curling around the chair cushion behind his head. He wanted to say, *Take off your clothes too; get naked with me.* But Evan wasn't relaxed yet. He was still edgy, still had that air of nervousness, like there was danger here. He still seemed to need to be in control.

But he wasn't rough. He'd learned Mal's rules too, untold. He knew that Mal had no taste for pain or harshness. Evan kissed and stroked him, searching and soothing, running his hands over Mal's ticklish hip bones, up his ribs. He brushed his fingers over Mal's nipples, making him squirm and whimper. When he gently pinched them, Mal had to break the kiss to gasp for air, throwing his head back. He might come, just from that.

Evan ripped open a condom packet, and Mal was disappointed. He didn't have anything, and he dreamed of Evan's wet mouth, without barrier. But condoms had been one of Evan's first hard rules, so he kept quiet, panting, as Evan rolled the latex onto him.

"*Ah,*" he gasped, as Evan swirled his tongue around the head of Mal's cock, strumming the tiny harp string there. Mal closed his eyes as ecstasy washed through him, washing away his frustration. He sank into sensation, entrusted himself absolutely to Evan's mastery, and was ravished.

Then it was his turn on his knees, with Evan fully clothed in the chair. Still hazy with pleasure, Mal rested his open mouth against slick latex, and waited.

Evan threaded his fingers into Mal's hair and pulled hard enough to sting, dragging Mal down on him as he thrust up. And then Mal's mouth and throat were stuffed full of cock, and he moaned.

Evan rolled his hips, slowly fucking Mal's face, going deep enough with each thrust to briefly stop Mal's breath. Mal sipped air on every downstroke, his mind blank and dizzy. His whole body was floating, tingling; he was only anchored by the bite of Evan's hands in his hair, the ache in his jaw as Evan owned his throat. When at last Evan's body tightened, bowing up from the chair, and his cock pulsed with release, Mal groaned again, exhilarated.

God, how he loved it.

"Damn," Evan whispered. The first word either of them had said since he'd rung the doorbell. "Damn."

Mal sat back on his heels, wiping his face. He cleared his throat rustily.

"Shit," said Evan. "Did I hurt you? Sorry, Mal."

Mal opened his eyes and looked up at Evan—sprawled in the chair, fully dressed except for his cock thrusting out of the fly of his jeans. Powerful and debauched, at the same time.

God, Mal wanted *everything*, wanted every inch of Evan's body to be his, wanted to touch him everywhere—

But it wasn't going to be that way. Not yet.

"*No problema*," he said casually, and rolled to his feet. "Anytime. Here, give me that thing, I'll toss it."

Evan wriggled out of the spent condom, and Mal got up and went, naked, to the kitchen. He tossed the condoms, said hello to Dulcie again, fetched a couple of beers out of the fridge—IPA for Evan, brown ale for himself—and went back into the living room where, to his great pleasure, he saw that Evan had taken off his jeans and was relaxing, eyes closed, on the floor, with his back against the sofa. He looked good, sprawled there on Mal's beige carpet in his T-shirt and boxers.

Mal sat on the floor beside him and handed him a beer.

"Thanks."

They drank quietly, and after a few minutes, Evan put a warm hand on Mal's shoulder, stroked his neck.

Ah, that was better.

"How was work?" Mal asked.

"Long. We let the new kitchen guy go."

"Oh? What'd he do?"

"The chef caught him sneaking sugar into the no-sugar desserts. For the second time."

"Horrors."

Evan grunted a laugh. "I know, but we've got diabetic people. We can't tell them something's safe to eat and then contaminate it. So anyway, then there weren't any no-sugar desserts, so the chef decided not to serve any dessert at all. Rather than have some for some people and none for other people."

"Probably a good call." Had Mal's mother been one of the deprived people, she would have been vocally displeased. And she didn't even like dessert. It was the principle of the thing.

"Maybe," agreed Evan. "But it didn't go over too well."

Mal closed his eyes, drifting with endorphins and happiness. Often when Evan came over, they'd blow each other and then he would leave. A few times, though—like tonight—Evan would relax enough to stay awhile. They'd drink beer together, talk about their day.

"How about you?"

"Um." Mal yawned. "Fine."

"What do you do all day?" asked Evan. "I assume it's not all trials, like *Law & Order*."

"Lots of paperwork." Evan shot a look at him, and Mal smiled. "No, really. Paperwork and assholes. There are so many assholes out there, and I see them all. Guys with no empathy, no sense of responsibility. Guys who think they're masterminds. The assholes kind of blur together." He was being flippant, but the seriousness of Evan's gaze cut through it. He added, "But, of course, I spend a lot of time with the victims, and the families of the victims, not the defendants. So my point of view is pretty skewed."

"You probably have to grow a shell," said Evan quietly. "Hearing people's terrible stories all day."

"Honestly, I do try not to. Every crime is individual, and every victim's story is important. You try to stay fresh and alive to every case, not get cynical. It can be hard, though, when something goes wrong. The evidence wasn't gathered right, or you make a mistake, or the jury doesn't see it. The guy walks, and you have to face the victims after. But that's how it goes."

"They're not all assholes though," said Evan. "What about the guys who are, you know, victims themselves? Addicts or mentally ill or something?"

That was a very *Evan* question. He liked to take care of people. "Oh, that too," agreed Mal. "A lot of them are." He paused. "So, yes, if there's an appropriate treatment program or hospital for a person like that who's committed a crime, I'll try to route them there, if I can."

Evan's eyes were steady on Mal. What did he think of Mal's work? Because Mal did not take care of people, not the way Evan did.

Mal said, "I want to be compassionate. The bad prosecutors, the ones who cheat, the ones who treat it like a game and winning is the only thing that matters? They're the ones who forget to be compassionate. But I represent the people, not the defendants. My job is to keep the public safe from people who are dangerous. Mostly they go to jail, and I've done my job. I know that isn't always the best thing for them, but I can't fix that."

"I could never do your job," said Evan.

"Hey, right back atcha."

Evan finished his beer, and Mal thought he was going to get up and leave; but instead he shifted, rolled onto his belly on the carpet, his head pillowed on his crossed arms. Mal lay on his back beside him, shoulder just touching his.

Maybe someday they'd cuddle. Mal loved to cuddle after sex.

Don't push.

Evan nudged him. "What happened with that case? The day I saw you downtown? You seemed upset."

"Oh, God, that was a clusterfuck," sighed Mal. "I think I told you about that case once—this guy kidnapped his ex at gunpoint, brought her home, raped her. He left her tied to a chair when he went to take a shower, and she broke free and ran to her sister's house. He said it was consensual ex-sex that got rough. I *so* wanted to put that guy away."

"But it got dismissed?"

"Layla died. The complainant. Nothing suspicious—a drunk kid ran a red and hit her in a crosswalk. Random fucking bad luck. Without her testimony—" Mal waved a hand in frustration. "I *tried* to make a case. We could have gone to trial with the sister's testimony and the medical evidence. We'd just have to be careful about hearsay. We could have . . . But nobody but Layla saw the gun, and without her to tell the story, the judge decided we didn't have enough."

"You're sure he did it?"

"Oh, he did it," said Mal grimly. He sighed, rubbing his chest with his fingertips. "The standard of proof is high for a reason—it's designed to prevent us from convicting an innocent person. There has to be so much evidence, so little doubt. But then a fucker like that one slips the net . . ."

This had gotten *heavy*, he thought, still massaging his heart.

He was willing to tell Evan anything though, even the bad stuff. Even about Zach, if he wanted to know. That first conversation in the bar had set the tone. Evan had told Mal a lot, and ever since, Mal had been willing to share.

Still, the conversation was too heavy. He wanted Evan to feel comfortable here. Perhaps then he would stay a little longer.

He rolled onto his side and propped his head on his hand. "New topic," he said playfully. "Tell me about the girlfriend. Or was it girlfriends?"

Evan's eyes opened, and crinkled with a smile. "Only one. Shanna. I was eighteen. But she was my girlfriend for, hmm, maybe five months? My longest relationship."

"What's it like?"

"What?"

"With a woman."

"You've never been with a woman?"

"Nope."

"It's not all that different," Evan assured him. "Just, you know."

"No, Doyle, I don't know. That's why I'm asking. Are you attracted to women?"

"No, hardly at all. I mean, she was pretty and she smelled good. But she—she didn't make me crazy."

Mal laughed. "Yeah."

"I really *tried*," Evan said, his brow furrowing plaintively, and they laughed together. "I know it seems funny now, but I tried so hard to get into it. It honestly wasn't all that exciting, though."

Mal's eyebrows quirked. "Then why do it?"

"She was nice," Evan said inadequately. "She— So I was in foster care until I turned eighteen, and my foster parents made sure I got therapy. They were good people. I met Shanna in a therapy group. For trauma survivors." For some reason this made Evan blush. It was cute.

"That's where everyone sits around and talks about their feelings?"

"Basically, yeah."

"I don't think I would enjoy the public lancing of wounds."

"It's more helpful than it sounds. Sometimes. Anyway." Evan closed his eyes again, resting his cheek against one strong forearm. "I was mixed up about sex, after what happened, and I sort of was thinking that I might try being straight."

"Really?"

"I was scared, but she wasn't scary. She seemed safe. And, you know, I was a teenager. I was so horny some days it seemed like a strong wind could get me off. Shanna was sweet, and little, and she liked me, and she was super-open about exactly what she wanted. I felt safe with her. So . . ."

"How was the sex?"

"Well." He smiled in the dark room. "Based on this one woman, I have to say that all the straight-boy drama about how hard it is to give a woman an orgasm is pure bullshit. The clit isn't very big, but it's *right there*. You can't miss it if you bother to look for it."

"While I *do* enjoy assuming that straight boys are sexually incompetent, in this case I think the testimony of one witness might not be sufficient evidence. So you, what, gave her blowjobs?"

"That's not what it's called with girls, but yes. She returned the favor." Mal raised his eyebrows, and Evan grinned. "Oh, sure. Girls know how to do it."

"Another myth destroyed."

"And also we had sex."

"You had penetrative sexual intercourse with a woman."

"Uh-huh." Evan was still grinning at him. "One man, one woman, just like in the movies."

Mal flopped back on the carpet, trying not to be jealous of poor beardy Shanna, who had been allowed to hug and touch and make love to Evan. "So what happened? Why'd you split up?"

Evan sighed. "Well. I mean, I was *gay*. I was fantasizing about dudes when I was in bed with her. That didn't seem very cool. More than that, though—I wasn't helping her."

He stared off, as if lost in memory, and Mal lay beside him patiently, waiting for the whole story. After a moment Evan went on, "She was in that therapy group for a reason, you know? And she wasn't . . . she was helping me. She was giving me something I needed, but it wasn't doing her any good. She was still cutting herself, and doing the binge-purge thing when she thought no one would notice. She believed she needed to have sex with people for them to like her, and I sort of realized that I was— I was not deliberately hurting her, but maybe I was hurting her. Or she was using me to hurt herself. Or maybe she just wasn't able to say no to me." He rubbed his forehead. "I don't know. It started to feel bad."

"I'm sorry," said Mal quietly.

"It's okay," said Evan, letting his hand flop back to the carpet. "We were kids. I bet a lot of kids have fucked-up relationships."

"I can confirm that," said Mal. "I wonder where that girl is now."

"She lives in Eureka. She married a tattoo artist a couple years ago. They can't have kids, but they're trying to adopt. What?" he said, when Mal blinked in surprise. "Of course I'm still in touch with her. She was mad when I broke up with her, but she's a very sweet person."

"You're a pretty sweet person too," said Mal.

But no, that was too far. Too affectionate, too intimate. Evan said, "Don't be stupid." He heaved himself up from the floor and began getting back into his jeans.

Damn.

Mal got up too, walked him to the door, and kissed him goodbye. And then returned to the living room alone, picked up the beer bottles, straightened the room. Wished he hadn't said that. Wished he hadn't forgotten that, to Evan, this was only sex, and compliments weren't welcome. Wished he wasn't going to bed alone.

CHAPTER ELEVEN

Evan stood on Mal's doorstep, Dulcie at his heels. He rang the doorbell.

It was about 10 a.m. on a Friday in November, and no sexy text had brought him today. Mal wasn't answering his texts or calls. Or the doorbell. Hunching his shoulders against the cold drizzle, Evan rang again, and then pounded the door with his fist for good measure. Still no answer.

For the first time, Evan used his key and let himself into Mal's town house.

Yesterday he'd worked an unexpected double shift at Cedar Heights—Jackie's kid had a broken arm, this time—and just as he'd been about to go home at nine, Dorothy Wallace had hit the emergency call button. He'd stayed all night with her, which meant he had now been awake for more than thirty hours. He needed to go home, shower, eat, and take his pills, but he was worried. Mal hadn't been answering his phone, and a check with Caro had revealed that he hadn't made it to work this morning, and hadn't called in.

Mal's town house was dim and still; it felt empty. Evan paused, listening. Nothing.

It smelled like sickness in here. Vomit.

"Mal?" he called.

No answer.

He toed his shoes off, dropped his messenger bag, pointed Dulcie to the kitchen rug, and padded across the living room and up the stairs.

Mal's bedroom. He'd never actually been in this room before; they'd always hooked up in the downstairs living room, on the couch, on the floor, against the wall. One memorable occasion on the dining room table.

The bedside lamp was on. The king-sized bed was unmade, empty, a tangle of sheets. The bad smell was strong in here.

Evan found Mal in the master bathroom, curled on the hard tile floor, perfectly still, wearing only his underwear and a T-shirt. Biting his lip, he crouched next to Mal and touched his fingertips to the pulse point beneath his jaw. Mal was warm; his heart thumped, strong and regular. He was asleep.

There was vomit in the toilet, in the wastebasket, on the toilet seat. A little on the floor. *Poor Mal.* Evan's touch went from clinical to caressing, and he reverently stroked the sweaty hair back from Mal's face.

Mal's eye opened. The dark iris rolled in its socket to look up at Evan.

"Hey there," said Evan. "Looks like you're having a terrible day."

"Fuck off."

Oh. Mal was going to be one of *those* patients.

"Okay," Evan said. "But first let me tell you something."

"Bite me."

Yep. Lots of people got ugly when they were sick. Evan shouldn't be terribly surprised to find that Mal was one of them. "Mal. You have food poisoning. The dinner you and your mother shared last night at Tsang's had gone bad."

Mal was quiet for a moment, then asked huskily, "Is my mom okay?"

"She was sick too, but now she's fine. Last night she rang for the nurse, and we stayed with her the whole time. She was sleeping when I left, but before she went to bed, she asked me to come check on you." *Demanded* might be a better word.

"She has an enlarged heart."

"I know. We're monitoring it. Not a blip."

"Good," said Mal, closing his eyes. "Thank you for letting me know. You can go now."

"Sure." Evan reached over Mal's head to flush the noisome toilet. "First, let's get you out of that pool of puke you're lying in, okay? I'll be right back."

He went to get his bag of supplies from downstairs and a clean T-shirt out of Mal's bureau.

Mal cursed him savagely and comprehensively while he pulled off his stained T-shirt, wrangled him into the clean one, wiped his face with a damp cloth, and mopped up the floor. "Put your arms around my shoulders," he said. "Let's get you back to bed."

"Let's not," snarled Mal, struggling. "Evan. I don't want you. Not your dick, and not your pity. Now get the fuck out."

Evan nearly said, *Fuck you too*, and walked out, leaving Mal on the floor.

He unclenched his jaw and took a deep breath. Shook it off. He had a job to do here.

Evan was strong and experienced at moving people in and out of beds, but he probably wasn't strong enough to get Mal off the floor without his cooperation. And besides, there was a limit to any nurse's bedside manner. If Mal wanted to stay on the floor, he could stay on the floor.

"All right," he said. He settled Mal onto the bathroom rug, tucking a folded towel under his head for a pillow. Then he got up, went to the sink, and began to scrub his hands. "Before I go, tell me one quick thing. Do you have any allergies?"

"Mangoes," mumbled Mal.

"Okay. No mangoes for you. You take any medication? Any pills?" Mal grunted, negative. Evan reached for his messenger bag and pulled out a box of medicated patches. He tore one open, sitting cross-legged on the floor beside Mal again.

At the sight of it, Mal gave a convulsive heave, trying to sit upright. "What the fuck is the matter with you?" he demanded hoarsely. "I want you *out*. I'm not a child and you are not a doctor. If you give me medication without my consent I will sue you until your ears bleed."

In a way, it was almost funny—Dorothy had *also* threatened to sue, when she was feeling at her worst. It didn't hurt when she did it. Evan shouldn't let Mal's anger wound him either—they were just no-strings sex partners. But perhaps that wasn't quite true anymore, because hurt was radiating through his chest.

Or maybe he was just tired. He couldn't remember when he'd eaten last. But this asshole was Caroline's best friend, and Evan was going to take care of him.

He summoned his patience. "You're right," he said to Mal, quietly. "I am not a doctor, and you have the right to refuse medical care. I'm going to give you information and ask for your consent, and I'm going to respect your wishes. Now shut up a minute, okay?"

In the face of Mal's indignant silence, he held up the patch. "This is over-the-counter medicine for nausea. You can buy it in any supermarket. It's in a patch so you can't ralph it up. It would help steady your stomach. The main side effect is drowsiness. Do you want it?"

Mal glared at him with bloodshot eyes, visibly wrestling with stubborn resentment and desire for relief. Then he seemed to run out of strength, nodded, and collapsed back onto the tiled floor. *Good boy*, thought Evan, but was smart enough not to say it aloud. He shifted Mal, gathering him closer and resting his head on his thigh. Then he peeled the backing off the patch and pressed it to Mal's deltoid, stroking to affix it to the warm smooth skin there. Mal sighed.

"Now," Evan said, holding up a clear bag attached to an IV tube. "This is *water*. It's got some electrolytes in it. Most of how bad you feel right now is due to dehydration. You could just drink water, but I'd like to give it to you in a drip so we know it'll stay down. Do you consent to that?"

"Okay," breathed Mal.

"Okay." Evan took Mal's hand, stroked his forearm. "Make a fist. Nice. You've got nice veins."

"Bet you say that to all the patients," mumbled Mal.

"No, I don't." Evan swabbed a vein with an alcohol pad, and slid in the needle, fast and easy. A little dressing tape to secure the needle, and another scrap of tape to stick the saline bag to the wall above his head. He checked the line to make sure it was flowing cleanly, and shifted, cradling Mal's head. "That's all, Mal. Go to sleep if you like. You'll feel better when you wake up."

Mal relaxed against him, the last bit of resistance draining away. "Okay," he whispered. "I hate this."

Evan stroked Mal's head and neck. "I know. Go to sleep, Mal."

For the next forty minutes, Evan sat cross-legged, back to the bathroom wall, watching the saline bag slowly flatten. Mal slept, curled on his side with his head in Evan's lap, and Evan rested his hand on Mal's neck, focusing on his steady pulse, his regular breathing.

So a patient had been mean to him. Mr. Willison was mean to him every day. He could shake it off. It was just illness talking—illness, and the humiliation that came with being ill. He knew this.

Knowing was good enough when it was Mr. Willison being hateful. It wasn't good enough now, though. It was different, when the hatefulness was coming from Mal.

Whatever. Do the job, same as with anyone.

When the bag was empty he replaced it with a new one. At some point Dulcie padded up the stairs. She stood in the bathroom doorway, gazing at Mal and Evan, eyes inquisitive, black nose working. Evan patted the floor. She lay beside him and rested her chin on Mal's waist. Evan stroked her head and dozed.

After the third saline bag, Evan stirred himself. It was afternoon. Both Mal and Dulcie were fast asleep. Mal seemed so sweet when he slept.

Evan removed the needle tidily from Mal's arm, swabbed a bead of blood away, slipped the folded towel under Mal's head, creaked to his feet. "Stay," he said to Dulcie.

Nursing was not very glamorous work. Not heroic or life-saving, generally. A lot of what he did was just cleaning up the messes the human body made when it was sick or injured. Smelly, dirty work, work that sick people couldn't do for themselves.

But he liked to do it. It helped people heal, and it restored their dignity a little. It was good, and necessary, to have someone be kind to you when you were at your weakest. He'd always prided himself on his commitment to that ideal.

He washed his hands, disposed of the IV and bags, washed his hands again. He stripped the bed, and started a load of laundry. Washed his hands yet again, and made up the bed with clean sheets. When he returned to the bathroom he found that the fluids he'd pushed had done their job: Mal was awake and unsteadily on his feet, clutching the bathroom vanity and brushing his teeth.

"Feeling better?"

Mal emitted a hostile grunt and ducked his head under the faucet. Evan remained nearby as Mal scrubbed water through his hair, in case he fell. When he straightened and shambled, dripping, toward the bedroom, they avoided each other's eyes in the mirror.

Mal mumbled, "A lot better now. Thank you," and collapsed into bed.

Evan helped him get under the covers, then toweled his wet hair. After he was sure Mal was fast asleep, he whispered, "You're welcome. You stupid jerk."

He found Mal's cleaning supplies and scrubbed the bathroom thoroughly, to kill any lingering bugs, and to get the smell of sickness out of the air. He cracked the window in Mal's bedroom, letting a trickle of cool fresh air in. The washer buzzed, and he put the wet laundry in the dryer.

When he was done, he checked on Mal one last time, nodded to himself, and left. From his truck, he called Caroline and let her know the situation. "He's healthy and young. He ought to bounce back from this no problem. You should go over there tonight after work though, try to get some soup into him. Make sure he's okay. If he does continue to be sick, he should probably go to the hospital."

"What about you?"

"I'm beat. Gotta eat something and get some sleep. Just to warn you, Mal's a teensy bit bitchy when he's not feeling good."

"Oh, I know. I've seen him hungover. He once called me a yapping Chihuahua."

"Did he," said Evan flatly.

"He lashes out when he feels vulnerable. He was sorry afterward."

"So that makes it okay?"

"Yeah, it does," she said, firmly. "Don't worry about Mal. I'll bring him pho."

Even more irritated than before, he hit a drive-through to pick up a chicken sub and ate it as he drove home. Dulcie was too polite to beg, but she sat attentively, and he let her lick the mayo off the paper wrapper when he was done. At home, he fed her and then showered. Aching with tiredness, he thought about crawling into bed, but Dulcie was staring at him with needy eyes. She'd been at Cedar Heights for thirty hours too.

So he put on his boots and, ignoring the bruised feeling in his chest, began to hike up to the top of the ridge behind his house. Dulcie ran ahead, off-leash. It was about three miles and eight hundred feet of elevation, a steep narrow dirt trail through hemlock and red cedar and alder that led to a rocky outcrop with a great view. As usual—and they did this hike once a day if weather permitted—the clear mountain air seemed to blow through his cluttered brain, stilling the restless cycle of worry. He sat on the rocks at the summit and looked north, where in the distance he could see the Columbia River in its gorge, wide and flat and blue. Solitude and exercise almost always helped clear his mind.

"I don't want you. Not your dick, and not your pity. Now get the fuck out."

That stung, even in memory. Like a slap.

Suppose, hypothetically, there was a couple, and one half of the couple said *fuck off* and *what the fuck is the matter with you* and *get the fuck out* to the other half. Could they continue as a couple after that? Was that a thing that relationships could recover from? He had no idea.

And, of course, he and Mal weren't actually a couple, were they?

But he didn't want to lose it—this relationship, whatever it was. He'd tried to keep it on a purely physical plane, but it wasn't just sex, not for him. He had come to feel that he could share anything with Mal, that he could trust Mal not to judge or criticize. But Mal's words— *"I don't want you, get out."*—brought him up short. In spite of himself, he had trusted that it was more than sex for Mal too.

He wondered what the next time he spoke to Mal would be like: Would they argue? Would he tell Mal to go to hell? Would Mal even care, if he did?

He didn't have long to wait; just as he reached home, his phone rang. He considered not answering it. It was getting dark, and he wanted to go straight to bed. But the call was from Mal. Evan looked at the name on his phone screen for a few breaths, then answered it.

"Hey," he said, leaning on the porch rail. "How are you feeling?"

"Better. Thank you for coming over. For what you did." Mal's voice was formal. Polite.

"No problem."

"And thank you for taking care of Mom. I just talked to her."

"You're welcome."

"Caro was here. Thanks for sending her to check on me."

"Sure," said Evan.

"And." Mal took a deep breath. "I am really, really very sorry."

Caroline said it was enough for her, when Mal was sorry. But it didn't feel like enough. Evan was so tired that he wasn't even sure *how* he felt. "For what?"

"For being such a shitty bastard to you," Mal said immediately. "I shouldn't have talked to you that way. You didn't deserve it, and I apologize."

Evan hummed. Mal certainly seemed sincere. It didn't make the knot of resentment and hurt around Evan's chest loosen though. Would a person in a relationship accept that apology and move on? "I'm a pro," he temporized. "I know it's hard to be sick. Don't worry about it."

"Oh, fuck. You're really mad."

You could say a lot of things about Mal, but *dense* wasn't one of them.

"Fuck," Mal said again. "Evan. Listen. I said— I mean, I think I implied that if you weren't there for sex, then you shouldn't be there. That was ugly, and despicable, and not true. I don't want you to think . . . *In* food poisoning *veritas*, you know?"

Evan's knees felt weak. He sank down to sit on the porch steps. "I know. I didn't think it was." A barefaced lie. That was exactly what he'd thought. "A lot of sick people say things they don't really mean. Your mom said she was going to burn Tsang's to the ground. I'm assuming she didn't mean that."

"Yeah, well, if Tsang's goes up in flames within the next few months, we never had this conversation." Mal sounded a little more relaxed now. "So you forgive me?"

Maybe they were okay. But Evan found that he couldn't let it go quite that easily.

"Actually, I kind of need you to not talk to me like that again. I know you were sick, and I know you and Caroline have this harsh banter thing—"

"No—"

"But that's not my thing, and I don't— It didn't feel good. I'm not so good at shrugging it off."

"You shouldn't have to." Mal's voice went soft. "I didn't want to be a patient to you. I didn't want you to think of me like that." He paused, then laughed with apparent embarrassment. "I *don't* want you to think of me like that. But I was terrible, and I'm sorry. I will not do it again. Please say you forgive me."

Mal really cared what Evan thought of him? Evan laughed shakily. *I really care what you think of me too.* "Yes," he said. "Of course I forgive you."

"And you'll come over?"

"What, tonight?"

"I'm better," said Mal. "I took a shower. I'm clean and I smell good. I'm not gross and vomity anymore."

Evan hesitated. It was over a half an hour's drive to Mal's house from here, in good traffic. He thought longingly of sleeping in his own bed.

"I want to replace your last memory of me with something nicer," said Mal, his voice low and persuasive. "Please, Evan. Come over. I want to see you."

Come over. I want you.

"I'll be right there," said Evan.

Mal kissed him at the door. He tasted like cinnamon mouthwash, and his lips were tender, sweet as honey.

Evan stumbled inside, kicked the door closed behind him, and fell helplessly into him. Arms around Mal's waist, Mal's open mouth sliding against his, and the day's frustration and worry flared and burned away, like a moth in a campfire. The gentleness of Mal's mouth was too scary though, so Evan grabbed his head and deepened the kiss, roughening Mal's face with his beard stubble.

"Upstairs?" Mal breathed.

They blundered up the stairs to Mal's room, kissing. Evan was giddy, laughing when their legs tangled. "Ow," breathed Mal when they bounced off the wall of the hallway, and they laughed again. When they got to his room, Mal stripped off his clothes, naked in a second, and flopped back on the bed, eyes closed, cock stretched long against his abdomen. Evan gazed at him while he pulled off his own clothes and kicked out of his jeans. By the time he lay down beside Mal, he saw that Mal's cock was softening, his body relaxed. *We'll just see about that.* He crawled on top of him, pressing his thigh between Mal's legs, rubbing against him, but Mal only hummed, turned into him, nuzzling his body.

Evan looked down at him.

Mal's muscles were lax, his breathing even.

Of course. He'd been sick. He'd had a momentary, illusory energy surge after he'd eaten, but his body still needed to recover.

Mal, his face blank and innocent, had fallen asleep.

Bad nurse, thought Evan, collapsing back onto the bed in defeat.

In spite of his frustration, he felt himself sinking into the soft bedding. Reclining for the first time in far too many hours, Evan's joints seemed to realign themselves. This bed was so comfortable. The mattress was firm, and the sheets were nice and smooth. They felt good against his skin. Slowly, the tension in his muscles bled away.

He closed his eyes. Just for a moment.

Evan was warm when he woke up, over ten hours later. Almost too warm, but profoundly comfortable and sporting a hard-on like a brick. Something heavy and hot was folded around him, making him sweat. Drowsily he opened his eyes.

He was in Mal Umbertini's bed, being snuggled by Mal Umbertini.

Mal's breathing was still slow and deep with sleep. His body pressed all along Evan's back, his knees tucked into the crook of Evan's legs, an arm thrown heavily over Evan's rib cage. His almost-snores whuffled softly against Evan's shoulder.

Evan looked down at Mal's hand, the long fingers loosely grasping his arm.

He'd never experienced much physical affection with his lovers. When he'd started having sex, it had been a hurried compulsion to get off, not to embrace. And later . . . well.

Evan took his own emotional temperature. He was fine. Better than fine, this felt good. He wasn't scared or even nervous.

He'd touched people before. Hugged, sometimes. Usually women. As with everything, it was better with Mal.

He closed his eyes, breathed deep, and let himself remain still. Peace poured over him like cool water. It was so good to lie in a man's arms. In his sleep, Mal was giving Evan pleasure so sweet, it almost brought tears to his eyes. He surrendered to it, to the press of Mal's chest against his back, the weight of his arm. He had been so starved for touch, all these years, and he hadn't even known it.

He dozed.

He woke again when Mal stirred. Mal's cock was now upright and questing against Evan's buttock like a dowsing rod arcing toward a spring. At the sensation, Evan's sprang eagerly to life again as well. Mal's breath hitched as he woke and seemed to register their relative positions. Evan didn't move, breathed tranquilly. What would Mal do?

After a moment's hesitation, Mal carefully disentangled his body from Evan's, and peeled away.

But Evan didn't want to lose contact with him. Impulsively, he rolled over and knelt on top of Mal, pinning him to the mattress, his knees between Mal's spread legs. Their noses bumped and their cocks brushed together. Morning breath, stubble. Evan gazed down into Mal's surprised and sleepy eyes, wanting more—not just sex, but more intimacy, more of this connection—and not sure how to ask for it.

Then Mal wiggled his eyebrows and lifted his hips, lasciviously rubbing himself on Evan's thigh. Evan's dick was as hard as a pistol and it pressed down into Mal's abdomen.

Mal smiled and silently raised his open hands, like he was responding to a stickup. Invitation, in Evan's language.

Evan was torn, for a second: doubt and mistrust, warring with his longing to be closer to Mal. He leaned down, clumsy with eagerness, and kissed him. Their tongues tangled, bodies humped together, uncoordinated, good but not good enough. He felt a syrupy smear of pre-come on his abdomen and grunted, rubbing harder.

He had no idea what he was doing.

Mal, now flat on his back, reached out a long arm to the bedside table, blindly opened a drawer, and used his fingertips to hook a plastic bottle, then handed it to Evan. Evan sat up, knees splayed, Mal's thighs draped over his, and poured a stream of almond-scented oil into his palm. He watched Mal's face as he wrapped his slickened hand around their cocks. *Like this?* Mal's lips parted in a gasp. *Yeah.* Grinning with pride, Evan firmed his grip. Mal thrust his hips, and his dick slid, long and hard and slippery, along the whole length of Evan's.

The sensation was unbelievably electric. Evan gulped for breath. Mal groaned hoarsely, and clutched the edges of the mattress in his hands.

Evan closed both slippery hands tighter around their paired cocks, and the flushed head of Mal's dick vanished and reappeared as he began to fuck the channel he'd made.

This was too good. Evan kept still and filled his eyes with the glorious sight of Mal Umbertini getting off.

Sometimes, when they were using their mouths on each other, they deliberately made it last, brought each other to the brink of orgasm and tried to stay there. Not this morning, though. Mal was going for it, seemingly single-minded with pleasure, driving toward completion, and he was magnificent in his abandon. His face was absorbed, eyes closed, tendons standing out in his throat. His abs crunched rhythmically as he pushed his dick through the channel of Evan's hands. His heels dug in, and he began to cry out with every breath, a soft gravelly *ah, ah, ah*.

Evan bit his lip as Mal's body went taut, cords of his arms and chest standing up under his sweating skin, his eyelids squeezing tight. Creamy semen jetted out of him, fat surges of it spattering his stomach, chest, throat, filling Evan's nostrils with the salty animal scent. Electric excitement shocked down the length of Evan's spine, tightening his balls, his body right on the point of orgasm.

Just from watching Mal.

After a moment Mal's eyes opened languorously, and they stared at each other. Then Mal whispered, "Come up here."

Evan clambered up, and Mal slithered down, keeping his hands above his head. Evan knelt over his face and shakily fed the head of his dick into the hot cavern of Mal's mouth.

"Oh, fuck yes," he groaned, slowly sliding in and out, careful not to shove in too deep. The position they were in prevented Mal from bobbing his head, but he wasn't being passive. He hollowed his cheeks as Evan withdrew, swirled the tip of his tongue around Evan's slit. Evan cried out and pressed back in. "You're so good," he panted, sweat breaking out on his shoulders. He wasn't going to last long. He gripped the base of his cock with one slippery hand and began to pump himself while Mal worked on his head. "So good." His hips stuttered, muscles tightening, as his awareness narrowed to the intense center of his need: his own hand on his cock, the heat and palpitation of Mal's mouth on the crown. "You're so— I want—" Evan palmed his sac, brushed his fingers lower, ground them against the rim of muscle around his hole, the pad of one fingertip pressing in just as Mal sucked him hard. *I want to be yours*, he might have chanted aloud, as orgasm overwhelmed him like a wave. He cried out as his body spasmed, shot, and his come filled Malcolm's mouth. Mal swallowed, the muscles of his throat coiling around him, and Evan cried out again. *Want to be yours.*

Through long waves of delight, Mal held him in his gentle mouth, until after several heartbeats Evan got oversensitive and pulled away.

Clumsily he clambered off Mal and flopped beside him on the bed, boneless and panting in the sweaty, happy aftermath of a truly fantastic orgasm. After a moment he turned to Mal, his mouth open to say *Thank you*, or perhaps *That was wonderful*, or maybe even *I am so in love with you*.

But Mal was wiping his lips with the back of his hand, and—

Oh crap, semen. The words of love froze in Evan's mouth. "Augh." He pressed his forearm over his eyes. "No condom."

After a moment, Mal said incredulously, "Doyle? Something you need to tell me?"

"No," muttered Evan. The bed jounced as Mal sat up, and Evan said again, "No. I—I'm— Mal, I swear. I'm in health care, I get tested. I've been very safe."

He felt as well as heard the silence of Mal's response. He forced his eyes open, emerged from behind the safeguard of his arm. "Trust me. I wouldn't not tell the truth about this."

"I trust you," said Mal. "I don't have anything, either." After a long moment, he added, "So what's wrong?"

"Nothing," said Evan, weakly. "That was—that was good."

Mal snorted, which was honestly all the response that deserved. He got up and stalked to the bathroom.

Evan heard the shower start.

What could he have said, in answer to that question? The truth? *Oh, the condoms?* he might have said. *The condoms are just one of the bullshit ways I maintain a distance from the people I have sex with. Because I'm a coward. Oh, the condoms? A physical barrier to protect my emotional self, like a snail shell around my slimy pathetic sluglike soul.*

Oh, Mal. Oh, hell. Eloquent, prickly, generous Mal.

He had almost said *I love you* to Mal.

Why? Why had he almost said that?

Because he loved him. He loved him so much.

He was so fucked.

Five minutes later, Evan lay in Mal's bed, still listening to the shower.

He remembered a morning, a week or so after his rescue from Nez's basement bedroom, several days before he'd been taken in by his foster family. What a starved, brutalized kid he'd been: furious, terrified, alone. But for a week, when he hadn't been spilling his guts to cops and lawyers of various agencies, he'd been given medical care, regular meals, and the safety and solitude of a room at the Chula Vista Best Western. A week of security, sleeping, eating, sitting in the sun by the little kidney-shaped pool, watching his white skin turn tan and his black bruises turn green. And one morning he'd awakened to a teenager's perfectly normal erection.

He'd stared at it with horror. It was still happening, his body's drive for pleasure and release. Nez hadn't killed it after all.

The realization had filled teenaged Alex with despair. He hadn't wanted it, couldn't cope with it, that healthy young sexuality of his. Ever since the En—ever since his mother had seen him come to the En, seen what he did there, and made no protest—he'd felt fundamentally dirtied and debased. After what happened with Nez—that profound self-betrayal—no. No.

He was still struggling to cope with his dick. Long periods of abstinence were interrupted by brief meaningless encounters, and he always needed almost-ritualistic layers of protection to make him feel physically safe. More than that: emotionally safe.

Years of therapy had taught him a little acceptance. He'd learned techniques to help him fight or ignore the lies that depression and anxiety told. He wasn't unworthy, he wasn't unfit. He hadn't asked for the rape, and he deserved to move beyond the pain. His therapist had urged him to give himself permission to have a life, to be happy.

So: a life. With Mal in it. It was all so new to him, this thing with Mal, and it was precious. Maybe he was ready to do as his therapist said, and try to have a normal relationship. Pull out of his protective shell. He wanted that: wanted Mal as an actual friend, a part of his life, as well as a sexual partner.

But could he? He could talk to Mal about work, about Caroline, even about the legal technicalities of his past. But could he talk to Mal about what he'd done, how he'd felt, who he'd been? Would Mal want to know? Would it be fair to proceed without telling him everything? Would Mal be horrified?

The thought of that conversation made him cringe. No. He just couldn't do it. Because Mal valued strength, was impatient with weakness. Evan didn't think he could bear to let Mal see his hidden weakness, lest Mal despise him.

A shard of shame was still lodged in his heart, its poison leeching out into his bloodstream. He was in some ways still the humiliated, ravaged boy he had once been. He could tell himself otherwise, but in his heart he still knew: Mal might desire Evan. Might even like and enjoy Evan. But that was because Mal didn't know Alex.

Evan closed his eyes and spent one last moment in Mal's bed, surrounded by his smell, remembering the way it had felt to be held by him. Last time.

Finally he rolled out of the bed, sniffling, and began to dress in yesterday's scattered clothes. He needed to go home, to be alone.

In his haste to be away, he didn't hear the shower cut off. He didn't notice that Mal had emerged from his shower, hips wrapped in a towel, until he was right behind him.

"Going somewhere?" asked Mal.

"Where do you think you're going?" laughed Nez, as Alex struggled to get out from under him. Hands hard, body implacable, tone mocking.

The panic attack hit him like a train. Evan's breath stopped in his lungs. Terror spiked. His vision tunneled. He staggered away from Mal, tripped over something, and crashed into a wall. His heart raced. Waves of pain rippled through his chest as he gasped for air.

Mal was there, touching him, speaking. Evan slapped at Mal's hands, warding him off, and Mal retreated. Evan curled up against the wall, palms pressed to his heaving chest.

Mindfulness. Dulcie would help, but Dulcie was downstairs. He concentrated on the moment, the carpet under his bare feet, soft and a little scratchy. The stuccoed wall against his back, cool. He concentrated on breathing with his diaphragm, focused on the rhythm of his breaths, in slow, then out.

Gradually his breathing calmed. His head cleared.

But for a long moment, even though the panic passed, he dared not lift his head. Because Mal was there. Mal had just watched him fall to sniveling pieces over nothing. A perfect illustration of why Evan was not fit for him.

Finally, he opened his eyes.

Mal was sitting on the floor across the room, naked but for the towel, his elbows on his knees and his hands clasped in front of his mouth.

"Sorry," said Evan. "I'm okay."

"Sweetheart. What did I do?"

Sweetheart? No, no. Mal couldn't call him that. "Nothing, I'm fine." Well, no. He wasn't *fine*. He was profoundly humiliated and desperate to be away from Mal. "I'll be fine."

"Do you . . . do you want to take a shower?"

"Yeah," said Evan. "That would be good." He stood up, still shaking. He could walk into the bathroom, put a door between himself and Mal. Dulcie cried outside in the hallway, and he said diffidently, "Could you take my dog outside?"

"Sure," said Mal, still sitting on the floor. "You don't, um, need her?"

"No."

"Do you need me? I mean, anything—"

Oh God, if only Mal would just *go*. Leave him alone for a few minutes. He said, "What I really need is calories. I think I ate one sandwich yesterday—I don't know when I ate before that."

Mal smiled tightly. "Well hell, Evan, we can do that. How do you like your eggs?"

CHAPTER TWELVE

Mal sat across from Evan at his tiny dining room table, eating scrambled eggs and whole-wheat toast, drinking coffee. Neither of them said anything.

This should have been a perfect morning. He'd awakened with Evan's naked body in his arms. They'd kissed and made love, and it had been wonderful. And now here they were, having breakfast together with the morning sun streaming in through the window. Like a happy couple.

What would come next, for a happy couple on a perfect morning? A long walk with the dog? Maybe they'd go to the off-leash area at Mount Tabor Park. Lunch. Then, perhaps, back home for a movie on the couch. Talk, cuddles, more sex. A perfect lazy Saturday.

Pure fantasy. He was losing Evan.

Evan put away food joylessly, like it was a chore. Eyes on his plate. His face was drawn, puffy, his jaw dark with stubble. Mal had offered his razor, but Evan hadn't used it. As though, after everything they'd done and talked about together, sharing a razor was too much commitment for him.

Maybe it was.

What had this morning been like for *him*? His clearly stated contract broken. *Condoms, blowjobs, no hands. Don't push.* That had been the deal. Yet that had gone right out the window this morning. Mal hadn't intended to violate Evan's boundaries, but that was what he'd done. And though it had seemed okay at first, it had ended up with Evan crying in a corner.

Mal's fault.

The rapport they'd built over the last weeks—the sense of physical comfort, the mutual warm intimacy—had been cut off as though by a thrown switch, leaving Mal feeling abandoned. Out in the cold again.

He wanted to beg Evan to stay. He was stopped only by the conviction that begging would only accelerate Evan's exit from his life.

Instead he tried, "I'm sorry, Evan." The haunted gray-blue eyes lifted, but not quite enough to meet Mal's. "I broke your rules. I didn't understand the consequences. I—"

Evan said flatly, "It's not your fault that I had a panic attack." His tone was cool. "And *I* broke my rules. I lost track of my eating schedule. So don't worry about it."

That was spectacularly unpromising.

Mal asked, "Eating schedule?"

Evan finished the last of his toast, wiped his hands on a napkin. "I'm a recovering anorexic, Mal. If I'm busy or stressed I can stop eating and not even notice. It's sort of a coping mechanism, to make me feel like I'm in control, but it's a really stupid one, because it actually makes the anxiety and everything a lot worse in the long run. I keep a schedule of what I eat and when, to make sure I'm, you know, not starving myself, but the last few days have been out of whack. You startled me a little this morning. If I had normal blood sugar, it probably wouldn't have gotten to me like that. Not your fault."

"Oh," said Mal. "So, right now, you're unhappy because of that? Not because of me?"

Evan shook his head, his eyes still distant.

Bullshit.

But, with his apology rejected, Mal didn't know what else to say.

Evan asked, unexpectedly, "Are you still in love with him?"

"Who?" Mal followed Evan's gaze to the old snapshot of himself and Zach, posing in all their gaudy finery, on the wall. "Good Christ, no. Why would you think that?"

"It's the only decoration in this entire place," said Evan, shrugging slightly, mouth widening in what was almost a smile. "It must be important."

"That's not a picture of love. That's a picture of me being an idiot. I'm wearing liquid eyeliner in that picture," Mal added. "False eyelashes and a corset. It must have taken me three hours to look that bad."

"Because why?" asked Evan, getting up and pouring himself more coffee, turning his back to Mal. "Did he want you to?"

"I honestly don't even know if he did," sighed Mal.

Evan returned to the table and drizzled cream into his cup. The coffee was decaf. Mal didn't normally drink decaf, and he didn't take cream in his coffee. He'd stood in the dairy aisle of the grocery store just a few days ago, and picked out that carton of cream, hoping that Evan would someday stay long enough to drink coffee with him. Just like the beer in the refrigerator—the same kind Evan had ordered when they'd gone to Pettygrove's.

Now, watching Evan stir cream into his decaf, he was reminded of liquid eyeliner; how much he'd disliked it, how he'd put it on anyway.

Did Evan really want to know this story? Well, Mal had just seen Evan at what was surely his most vulnerable. Would an offering of his own most painful memory balance the scales a little? Make Evan more comfortable?

He said, "His name was Zach Muller. He was a force of nature. The sort of person who seemed big, even though he was only about five six. But everyone listened when he talked. If he suggested something, everyone would agree. He'd walk into a room and everyone would look up. He was like an attention gravity well."

"You do that."

"I— No." Wow, was that how Evan saw him? "No. I suppose I learned to project confidence from him, but he was . . . He hung out with a crowd of theater people and burlesque performers and drag queens, attention whores all, and he pulled them. Like a sun. And then there was me. I tagged along."

"I can't imagine you tagging along after anyone."

"You never met him." And Evan didn't know *him* that well if he found that so hard to imagine. Mal would have done anything for Zach. He had very little pride when he loved someone.

He went on, "Zach would stay awake for four or five days in a row, with coffee and Ritalin and cocaine, and make me stay up too. Suggest crazy shit that seemed like great ideas, coming from him. Pranks, trespassing, public indecency. Drugs, dares. And then he'd crash hard, drink warm champagne in bed, try to stay drunk and asleep for a week. During those times he'd only have sex in the dark, so I couldn't see him crying."

Mal paused; Evan was meeting his eyes for the first time this morning, his expression grave.

"I'd like to absolve myself by saying that I was too young to see the red flags, but the truth is that everything Zach did seemed brilliant and beautiful and right, because it was him doing it. Even when it was reckless, or cruel, or obviously fucked up. I can't explain it. My judgment was completely compromised. I just wanted to be close to him, and that was all I cared about." He smiled a little, sadly. "Do you ever look back at yourself, and think, 'Who was that dumb kid?'"

"Yes."

"That's what that picture is," said Mal. "A dumb kid, who should have done something. *Anything* would have been better than that . . . blind devotion. I found his body a few days after that was taken."

"Oh."

"He'd taken a lot of pills, and then hanged himself with one of those orange extension cords. The pills would have done it, they said, but the cord killed him first. He left a note, apologizing to his parents. Not to me. It didn't mention me."

Evan looked down into his coffee cup, his brows knotted, shoulders hunched. Pity? Or compassion? He didn't speak.

"I went to Zach's funeral." Mal wasn't sure why he was still talking—maybe to postpone Evan's departure. "I wasn't invited, I just showed up. His family lived in this little town on the Georgia border. Baptists. They couldn't figure out who I was, but they were too polite to kick me out."

The memory of that funeral always made Mal feel sick, even now—the helpless fury, the scorching grief that no one in that room could or wanted to understand.

"It was so weird. All these people, his family and childhood friends, standing around talking about him like he was someone I'd never met. His high school grades, and how good he was at baseball, and the time he won a spelling bee in, like, eighth grade. And I got angrier and angrier and angrier. I wanted to get up in front of that church hall and yell, 'I used to lick his asshole! He taught me how!'" Evan's jaw dropped open slightly, and Mal shook his head. "He taught me how to be gay in public, and not ashamed. He had a lip sync routine to 'True Colors' that made straight men weep. I was a toy to him, something that he used to distract himself from his pain, but at least I knew who he was."

Evan was staring at him. "Did you do that?"

"No." Mal managed a smile. "And I'm glad I didn't. They were just people trying to grieve. None of us knew how to do that. I don't think any of us knew how to get our heads around who Zach was and what he did. Who was I to say I knew him better than they did? I didn't know him at all."

"What did you do?"

He sighed. "Went back to Maryland. I'd already been accepted into university there, and I needed the in-state tuition. Lived with a cousin in Annapolis for a while until I got my financial aid in order." He shrugged. "Moved on."

Evan returned his gaze to the surface of his coffee. "But you didn't get over it," he said. "Not really. It's still part of you."

"Yes."

Mal remembered what Evan had said, once: *"I'm not going to get used to you, like a woodland creature eating an apple out of your hand."* For a quiet man, Evan sometimes produced the perfect turn of phrase. And of course he had been right: Mal had been luring Evan with sexual pleasure, hoping to teach him that he was safe in his presence, hoping to earn his trust. *Condoms, blowjobs, no strings, no promises, but give me a little more. Come just a little closer. Let me love you.*

Look how well that was turning out.

Evan took a deep breath and squared his shoulders.

Here it comes. Grief rose up from Mal's belly, into his throat. He pushed it down.

Finally Evan said, "I'm not going to come around anymore, Mal."

Damn it.

Something in Mal's nature demanded that he argue. Present all the reasons why Evan was wrong, and that what Mal wanted was right. He bit his cheek against the impulse, then said, "I'm really sorry to hear that. Will you tell me why?"

Evan looked out the window. The morning sun came out from behind the clouds and shone in, striking sparks of gilt from his gray-blue eyes. Mal had never noticed that before, those fine rays of silver, radiating from his pupils.

Evan said, slowly, "I don't think we're compatible."

"I disagree. You don't like the mint condoms, and I think the cherry ones taste like cough drops. So we trade, and it's all good."

Evan slanted him a reproachful look.

Okay. Serious. "I think we're very compatible."

"No, you don't," said Evan.

"Don't tell me what I think," said Mal mildly. "Yes, I do. I like what we do. I like all of it. I like what we're doing *now*. I'm not trying to pick your locks or demand anything of you. I don't need that. We can go right back to how we were before this morning, blowjobs and condoms. If that's what you want. Whatever you're comfortable with."

Evan was staring at him with those sun-struck eyes. Then he glanced away, out the window. He looked skeptical. Oh God, Evan didn't believe him.

There was no wrong thing to say at this point, nothing that could make it worse, so Mal might as well say what he needed to say. "I just want you, Evan. I just want to be with you. However it works. For as long as you want to. I care about you, and I don't want to lose you."

But he had lost him. Evan was flushed, eyes down. All systems stop. "No," he said. "I'm done. Thanks, though. We'll probably see each other around, because of Caroline, or at Cedar Heights. I hope it won't be weird. Don't text me again, okay?"

He got up, got his jacket. Whistled for Dulcie unnecessarily, because she was, as always, right there by his side.

Mal sat numbly at the table, staring at the photo of Zach, listening to his own heartbeat.

"Sugar, you're so serious about everything," Zach had mocked him. Still true.

Evan was opening the front door. He wasn't going to just *go*, without another word, was he? Mal got up and caught the door in his hand. They stood staring at each other. Yes, this was it.

He lowered his head, closing his eyes. After a moment's hesitation, Evan leaned in and brushed their mouths together.

A peck goodbye. Sweet, but still goodbye.

"Bye," said Mal.

Evan nodded. And then he was gone.

The day that followed sucked.

Mal's chest hurt. His eyes stung like someone had flung salt in his face. His stomach fluttered with a sensation like fear, or the return of his food poisoning. He couldn't escape the feeling of loss, couldn't talk himself out of it. How could you grieve for what you hadn't really had?

He needed distraction. So he went to the gym to go swimming, forgetting that Saturday was free swim day for families. He glared with displeasure at the children frolicking in the blue water, then went back home, changed, and went for a run. As he trotted past the Mount Tabor dog park where he'd wanted to take Evan and Dulcie, it began to rain.

He called Caro to see if she wanted to hang out with him, but she said she was spending the day with Paul. Maybe he should invoke best friend privilege and demand she ditch the boyfriend to comfort him? But then it occurred to him that maybe Paul was an excuse. She might actually be hanging out with Evan, and felt too awkward to say so.

He had other friends. Stuart would probably be up for something. But Stuart was a work colleague as well as a friend, and he didn't want to be like this in front of a colleague. Jay and Patrick would let him hang out, but ever since they got married, they tended to radiate monogamous joy in a way that made Mal almost ache with envy, and that was before he'd met Evan. Kieran would let him cry on his shoulder, but then he'd want to take him out and get him laid. No.

He considered paying a visit to his mother. Which was *ridiculous*. She wouldn't be there for him. She hadn't stood up for him on the day his father had thrown him out; she hadn't invited him to her wedding, hadn't reached out to him at all, not for years. Expecting her to comfort his broken heart was like expecting flowers to bloom on an iceberg.

Or maybe he was misjudging her? She had reached out, eventually, hadn't she?

He shook his head, pulled on a jacket, and went to a movie by himself, picking one at random. A buddy comedy that traded on knee-jerk gay panic for humor. After half an hour, Mal found himself tearing up in the dark, and left.

Finally he went downtown, keyed into the deserted courthouse, and did some work.

Evening found him back on Hawthorne Street, wishing he were drunk. He walked past Pettygrove's, where he and Evan had once shared beer and painful memories. "Always Something There to Remind Me" by Naked Eyes spilled out onto the pavement.

The algorithm in charge of *that* fucking playlist was apparently wired into the pain center of Mal's brain. He gritted his teeth and kept walking.

Closer to his town house was a sports bar called the Patera Zone, where the symbology of the Seattle Seahawks was prominently displayed, and the big-screen TVs all showed football games. On a whim he went in, perched at a little round table, and asked for a beer.

He sat there for hours. Nothing to remind him of Evan in the Patera Zone. Did Evan like football? Mal didn't know. He'd never had the slightest interest in sports, himself.

There were lots of male couples here, drinking and watching the TVs, though he was pretty sure they were mostly straight. Some women too, of course. The waitstaff was female and nubile, wearing Seahawks jerseys and tiny tight black shorts.

A game ended, and another one began. The Seahawks didn't seem to be playing on any of the screens, although the foursome of guys to Mal's left seemed very excited about the Denver Broncos. His pretty brunette waitress kept the beers coming. He kept his mind occupied with the music: classic rock of the feel-good variety. The Rolling Stones cried for shelter; ZZ Top growled suggestively about La Grange. Why weren't there more female classic rock acts? Mal kept drinking while he tried to think of some. Lita Ford. Patty Smyth. Pat Benatar.

What was Evan doing right now? Working on his house? Walking Dulcie? What else did he do with his spare time when he wasn't working or blowing Mal? Did he like to read? Collect stamps? They'd never gotten to know each other well enough for Mal to find out.

They never would. It was over. Evan didn't want him.

Mal had gotten about three-quarters of the way to thoroughly trashed when his waitress came by with his refill and said, "I'm going home for the evening, but Amber will take care of you."

"Okay, thanks."

She lingered at his table, eyeing him. He eyed her back with bleary surprise.

Women did not usually look at Mal the way she was looking at him.

Her football jersey said *SHERMAN*. He wondered if that was her name, or a Seahawk's. She had the kind of sleek, curvy body that most men would deem bangin'. He mentally took stock of what he was wearing: gray chinos, a heather-purple V-necked sweater vest over a button-down. Not exactly a "Love Wins" T-shirt, but amid this crowd of denim-clad bros, he surely looked nearly as effete and queer as he was.

Sherman's gaydar was terrible.

"Do you have a ride home?" she said.

"I live right over there," he said, waving his beer vaguely toward the door. "I'll walk. I'm fine."

"You seem pretty sad."

Alcohol, plus her sympathy, loosened his tongue. "I got dumped this morning. My fault. I screwed up, and I got dumped."

"I'm sorry," she said, standing hipshot, leaning on his table. Her voice took on a compassionate croon. "That's the worst."

"No, it's—" He stopped. He'd been about to say, *It's okay*. Instead he said, "Yes. It's the worst."

She propped her elbows on the table. "If you don't want to go home alone, I could keep you company."

He nearly choked on his beer. "Sherman, that is a truly breathtaking offer, but I wouldn't know one end of a woman from another."

Her self-confidence was admirable. She just smiled those glossy lips and said, "Maybe I could show you."

He laughed. Her smile widened. He said, "Why in the world would a lovely woman like you want to endure the incompetent fumblings of a depressed fag like me?"

"Don't call yourself that."

"Sticks and stones, Sherman. Answer the question."

She pursed her lips. "You don't stare at me. And you seem smart. Like someone I could talk to. You know, after."

Ah, yeah. That time after sex, when Evan's defenses dropped, and he was relaxed enough to talk. Before the defenses went up again, and he went home. A precious ten-minute window, sometimes fifteen. Before Mal had fucked it all up.

"No, I'm done," Evan had said. Not unkindly. Not angrily. Just no.

"I'm an idiot, both before and after," Mal said, tiredly. "Mutual dissatisfaction guaranteed."

"You don't know that."

"I kind of do." He nodded toward the quartet of Broncos fans. "I'm guessing any one of those guys would welcome the opportunity, though."

Sherman's eyes slid toward the Broncos fans. Her chin went up with a little head toss, like a spirited filly. *I think not*, it said.

How had his glass gotten empty already? Hadn't she just brought this to him? He glanced around for the other waitress—Amber?—and Sherman leaned in, touching his hand. "Listen," she said. "They won't cut you off here until you almost pass out. But you should call it a night, okay? You've been here for hours. Go home and drink some water and get some sleep."

He gazed at her. "You're a nice person."

"I am," she agreed. "And don't drunk-call your ex."

"You're smart too."

"I know what I'm talking about. You've had enough." She patted his hand. "Go home."

He cashed out, tipping extravagantly. Back at home, he brushed his teeth, drank some water, and went to bed, waiting for the world to stop spinning.

In the dark, he took his phone and thumbed into the message bar, *I miss you.*

Deleting the text unsent, he closed his eyes, pressed his face into his pillow, and miserably hoped he could sleep.

CHAPTER THIRTEEN

A week after ending things with Mal, Evan was driving down Glisan in Troutdale, on the way to the grocery store. Caroline was coming over later to help paint his bedroom, and he needed to pick up some snacks. A dusty green Subaru Outback emerged from a side street and pulled into traffic one car behind him, and his scalp prickled. Had he seen that car before? When? Earlier in the week, on the way to work? Yesterday, on the way home?

Impulsively, he signaled right, then cut left across traffic into the parking lot of an office park. Totally illegal, but a tough maneuver to follow.

The Subaru continued on straight.

"What do you think?" he asked Dulcie, watching as the Subaru vanished in the distance. "Am I just being a nervous freak?"

He was. Nez was in prison. Icaza was dead. No one cared that he was Alex Farkas except people who loved him. He was in hiding for no reason, and had been for years.

He sighed and scratched Dulcie's flat head with his fingertips. "I hate being a nervous freak."

"I'm working on making it official," said Caroline, helping Evan carry cans of paint up to his bedroom. "The guy I talked to doesn't work for San Bernardino County anymore, so he couldn't look up your file, but he said that if there was a choice between prosecuting you for manslaughter, and protecting you as a witness to the drug ring, they'd have chosen the drug ring every time."

"Was there a choice?" he asked. "I mean, could they have closed the case without prosecuting me?"

"Sure," she said. "But for some reason they didn't. Maybe they left it open because they were planning to come back around to you. But then a new DA came in and the policy changed." She crouched beside him and watched as he pried the lid off a can and stirred the dark, shining gray contents. "I think they were sloppy. Mom's killer was dead—they could have closed her case, and didn't. Careless, mediocre work. My guy says the new DA reorganized the whole department because of stuff like that. Anyway, I'm working on getting them to close the cases. Derrick's and hers."

His hands shook a little as he poured the paint into a tray. "You know, getting arrested for murder is like the only thing I *haven't* worried about until now."

"They're not going to arrest you," she said confidently. "The statute of limitations for manslaughter has passed, so they'd have to go for premeditated murder. And they don't want to do that."

"How can you be sure?"

"Because the facts of the case don't fit that crime. And they'd lose."

"People go to jail for crimes they didn't commit. And I did kill Derrick."

"Don't worry, Alex. I promise you it's not going to happen."

"So it's over?"

"It's been over for a long time." Her shoulders had a dejected slump. "I just didn't know it. I'll let you know if you need to make a deposition, and I'll make sure you have a lawyer for it if you do. But yes, it's over."

"Okay." So long as he didn't end up in prison, these were relatively minor details to him—he had always known what had happened to their mother, had been living with it for years. For Caroline it was still new and painful, and the fact that the cases were still open clearly rankled like a splinter.

He dipped a brush into the paint. "You okay?"

"I will be. Ready?"

"Ready."

He stroked the brush onto his cleanly primed bedroom wall, then stood back to judge the stripe of gray. It looked dark and cold, shiny, like new asphalt.

"This looks like asphalt," said Caroline, beginning to roll paint onto the wall under the window.

"I think when it dries it'll be lighter."

"Why did you pick gray?"

He cut a line of paint along the seam where the wall met the steeply-sloping ceiling, satisfied with the way it covered up the white primer. "Well, I started out thinking about the master bath."

"The master bath that made me feel like I was having an acid trip?"

"That one, yeah." He laughed. "Three more paychecks and I'm ripping that shit out, so please enjoy it while it lasts."

"Oh, I think those orange walls will haunt my dreams even when they're gone."

"They had a lot of that orange paint. It was in the kitchen too. Anyway, for the new bathroom, I thought I'd take out the tub and put in a walk-in shower, and I was looking at these tiles that are like river pebbles. They're pretty, and they're kind of round and rough, so they're not too slippery to stand on?"

"Uh-huh?"

"So they're gray, but a warm gray, and sparkly." Caroline's eyebrows were up, and he added, "Not *disco* sparkly. Flecks of mica in the rocks, you know? Anyway, that's what made me think of gray for the bedroom too."

"You don't find it a little grim?"

"No, it'll be nice," he assured her. "It'll warm up when it's dry. White trim, white curtains. You'll see."

"Hmm."

"Hey, we can't all have pink chintz with big flowers."

That got a smile. "I love my pink flowery chintz."

"You know who else would have loved your pink flowery chintz? Mom."

She picked up her paint roller again and turned to the wall. "Did Mal tell you about the place he's been hanging out? The sports bar?"

Change of subject much? But then again—Mal Umbertini in a sports bar? "No," said Evan. "But I haven't seen him around much lately."

"You were pretty tight for a while."

"Yeah."

"But not so much now?"

"Nope," said Evan, his heart squeezing.

He was having second thoughts. It was foolish, because breaking it off seemed like the right thing—the only thing—to do.

But even so, he wanted Mal bad. He wanted just to see him, to have that sense of rightness he felt whenever they were together. Missing him was a black sorrow in his chest that wouldn't go away. He wanted to beg Mal to let him back into his life—*Love me and all my messy drama.*

But that was the problem, of course. Evan was a chronic emotional train wreck, and Mal had never signed on for that.

Evan thought of Mal's story of poor Zach Muller, which he maybe hadn't paid enough attention to at the time. From Mal's description, Zach had been suffering from mental illness—one different from Evan's particular constellation of symptoms, but a mental illness nonetheless. Some assemblage of pain and despair that had made it impossible for him to go on. But even though Evan was not Zach, surely, after experiencing the worst fallout of Zach's affliction, Mal would not want to cope with Evan's.

Mal had said they could go back to the way they were. No strings. Evan was tempted, because he desperately missed that too—the sex, and the touching. Maybe they could just do a casual thing, once or twice a week, and he could teach himself to be content with that. Sex, and a little conversation.

But that seemed like a terrible idea. He was trying not to give in to his self-destructive tendencies anymore. And it was painful even to imagine how it would be—loving Mal, and pretending not to. It would break his heart.

He wanted to confess to his sister how miserable he was, and ask her what he should do—but Mal was her best friend. He was afraid of what she'd say.

He was afraid he was about to find out. "So, the sports bar?"

"It's called the Patera Zone. It pretty much shows all the football games this time of year."

"Does Mal like football?"

"Not in the slightest. You should have heard him trying to explain it to me, like, 'There's actually a strategy to it, Caro, they're not just running into each other like bighorn sheep.'"

Evan bit his lip against a smile. "Uh-huh." He really wanted to ask, *What else did he say? Did he mention me? Is he mad at me? Does he think of me at all?*

"He's got a theory that it's called the Patera Zone because of the prevalence of knee injuries among football players."

"What?" That did make Evan grin. "I don't think that's right."

"Anyway, he's been working like crazy lately," Caro said, painting. "Going to the office on the weekend, coming in early, leaving late. I don't think he's sleeping very well. He's got dark circles under his eyes, and this morning he'd missed a spot shaving, which he *never* does. And then spending his evenings at the Patera Zone watching football."

"Uh-huh," said Evan again. She didn't say anything else, and he glanced over his shoulder to find her gazing at him, her eyes as blue as a summer sky and as pointed as newly sharpened pencils. "So," he said. "Did you ask him what's bothering him?"

"I thought I'd ask you."

"And you think I know?"

"I think you broke his heart," said Caro.

Evan's hand trembled, and he dripped paint onto the toe of his sneaker. "Shit. No way."

"Did you break up with him?"

He crouched to wipe his shoe with a paper towel. "Kiki. Yes, but we weren't, like, having a real relationship."

"Says who?"

"Well, him." Evan looked up at her. "And me. We discussed it. It was fun, it was casual, and now it's over. It was not a big deal."

"So Thanksgiving will be fine?" she pressed.

"Yeah. Of course."

"Because Thanksgiving is very important to me," she said. "And I've *always* spent it with Mal."

Thanksgiving was the day their mother had died, of course. The day they'd lost each other. And in Evan's absence, Mal was the family Caroline had chosen. Mal was the one she'd relied upon, to love and support her, to fill the gap where her lost brother had been. Evan had always spent it alone, walling himself up in solitude to get through it, but this year he was spending it with his sister. With them.

"I'm glad you had someone to spend Thanksgiving with," he said. "We're not enemies or anything, Kiki. We both . . . I don't want to make it hard."

They painted in silence for a few minutes. "Do you always do enchiladas?" asked Evan after a while.

"Oh, no. But it has to be a no-turkey day. No turkey, stuffing, cranberry sauce, *nada*. We've done sushi, takeout Chinese. Last year I made meat loaf."

"Every Thanksgiving was no-turkey day at the Farkas home," said Evan. He couldn't even remember what they'd been planning to eat that last Thanksgiving. They'd definitely planned something: they'd been deep in the Food Game by that time, and they ritualistically planned all their meals. Something involving canned chicken broth, probably, with bread and margarine and pickles. He'd eaten a lot of pickles back then, liking the strong sour flavor, and pickles had almost no calories. Maybe some yogurt for dessert, because it was a holiday.

"Yep," said Caroline soberly, probably remembering the same thing. "But Mal's whole family always got together and did some big terrible joyless turkey feast. Twenty people eating too much food, wishing they were somewhere else." She bent at the waist and dipped up more gray paint. "Our Thanksgiving ritual was never just for me, you know."

"His whole family? He's an only child, isn't he?"

"But he's got scads of cousins and uncles and aunts and grandparents. Half of them are strict Catholics, and the other half are icy WASPs. Everyone pretends to be a close-knit loving family because that's what you're supposed to do, but they secretly hate each other."

"Wow," said Evan. "Makes heroin-trash in Barstow sound relatively nice."

He was kidding, of course, and she tiptoed up to kiss his cheek. "He has his own scars," she said. "Different from ours, but still, he didn't have a great childhood."

"I know that."

"Holidays that insist upon the importance of family always get him down."

Evan nodded.

"So be nice to him."

"I *will*, God," snapped Evan. "I've never not been nice to him, Caroline."

She drilled him with a steady stare. "Really?"

Evan sighed. "We were perfectly lovely to each other."

"You're full of shit."

Evan met her eyes. "No, I am not," he said clearly. "We had a conversation. We discussed how our relationship was casual and not permanent, and if Mal's unhappy about how it turned out, it's not because he didn't know."

"Know what?" said Caro. "That you think you're damaged goods?"

"Stop it," whispered Evan.

They glared at each other, blue eyes into blue-gray, and then Evan asked, tightly, "Should I butt out on Thursday? I took the day off, but I can throw my tent in the truck and head for the beach? You and Mal can do your—"

"Alex, *don't*." She dropped her roller and came to him, putting her hands on his shoulders. "I just found you again," she said. "Don't make me spend another Thanksgiving without you. Don't make me choose between you and Mal."

"Then stop trying to make me— Stop thinking that I can—" The words clogged in his mouth.

She had no such problem. "Stop threatening to go away again when you don't like what I say!"

"I'm not," he said. "Not going to go away. Just—" He bit his lip, forced himself to speak clearly. "Stop thinking that Mal and I are going to fall in love and be a happy couple. Because I get how that would be cool for you, but it's not how it is."

Her lips pressed together. "I'm sorry," she said, in a quieter tone. "You and Mal, I know it's not about me."

"It isn't."

"But you're pretending you're fine and you're not. You're jumpy and anxious and not sleeping."

"Jumpy and anxious and not sleeping is actually sort of normal for me."

"You're sad."

He couldn't deny that.

"And Mal's sad."

"Just because he's discovered football doesn't mean he's sad." That sounded weak even to him.

"You know him well enough to not pay attention to his *face*, right?" Caroline said. "His face says 'I don't care,' but his heart is the size of the Pacific Ocean."

"Poetic."

"I am not kidding. People always think he's being sarcastic when he's telling the truth."

"I care about you, and I don't want to lose you," Mal had said. And Evan had looked at him and thought, *Seriously?*

Caroline put her hand on his nape. "If you don't feel anything for him, then I'll shut up. You're not obligated to care about him just because he's my friend. If you don't want to, I'm sorry. And I'll shut up. But if you do, and he does, and you're letting your neuroses about our mom and all that other horrible crap get in the way, then that sucks."

Evan's face was burning. *I do, I do, I do. But—*

"I'm sorry," he said to her shoulder. "But this thing I do, where I'm a basket case all the time? It doesn't go away."

"You're not a basket case."

"I totally am. Today I spent part of the morning driving around losing the guy who was tailing me, even though no one was tailing me. And I wish I could stop and be normal and have a boyfriend. But I can't. The anxiety is part of my brain now, and . . . and Mal doesn't need that in his life."

"Maybe Mal can decide what he needs for himself."

"Maybe Mal thinks he can fix me," said Evan. "Maybe he doesn't get that I'm not fixable. I killed a man with my bare hands, Kiki. I let guys use my mouth for money. I—I was— Don't," he said, helplessly trying not to cry as she wrapped her arms around him. "It's just, he's good, Kiki, like you told me, and I'm not, I'm not—"

"Yes, you are." She held him tight. "Yes, you are. You're good. You got put in an impossible situation, and did what you did, but you're good."

"Ugh, do you see what I'm doing right now?" He pulled away from her, blotting his eyes on his sleeve. "God. I *know* I don't deserve to be punished or anything, but it follows me around like this. I don't know how to be a normal person."

She put her hands on his face, wiped his tears with her fingertips. "Boxy, what do you think Mal and I have in common? We were both so broken and so bad at pretending to be normal people."

"Him?"

"Oh, yeah. Just as bad as us, and *he* never got therapy."

"I don't see him like that."

"Maybe he doesn't see you like that, either." Caroline went up on her toes again and hugged him. "Hey," she said soothingly, squeezing. "I'm sorry. I'm not trying to upset you. I think he likes you the way you are."

But he couldn't believe that. No. Evan looked down and saw that dark-gray paint was dripping from his brush and forming a pool on an unprotected bit of his hardwood floor. Plaintively, he asked, "Do you think we could just paint?"

CHAPTER FOURTEEN

Wednesday night after work, Evan went to the Patera Zone. There was no street parking near the bar, so he parked a block east on Hawthorne—in front of Mal's town house, in fact. The bar appeared to be packed, busy enough to upset Dulcie, and it was nice and cool out, so just this once he left her in the cab of the truck. She would sleep undisturbed on the passenger seat until he got back.

He stood on the street in the cold dark air, looking through the big windows. It was brightly lit and full of music and color and people. The wind blew stinging rain against his neck and he shivered.

What if it were true? That Mal's heart was broken. Because of him. What if it were true, that Mal really cared about him?

He stood in the cold and dithered about whether to go in.

Caroline didn't believe Mal wanted to save Evan. If he did—if he wanted to fix him—they would both be disappointed, because this was it. Evan was Evan. He'd accepted that his anxiety was something he'd have to live with, for always, and anyone in his life would too. But maybe Kiki was right. Maybe he just wanted to be in Evan's life.

Or maybe he just liked the sex. Maybe Evan loved a man who would never love him back. He would probably be better off walking away.

Oh, who am I kidding? He wanted to see Mal again. He wanted Mal Umbertini. He wanted whatever Mal was willing to give, and he wasn't strong enough to keep away.

He went into the bar as something important happened on the big-screen TVs, and the patrons erupted into loud baritone shouts of celebration. Evan glanced around nervously. None of the tragedies of his life had been the result of homophobia—as far as he knew, it wasn't even immediately obvious to most people that he was gay. But he still had the instinctive gay man's wariness of large groups of (he supposed) het sporting fans. He felt like a cat amid a pack of big, apparently friendly dogs.

No one was paying attention to him, though. Everyone's eyes were on the screens, which were showing—not football—some sort of sports trivia game? Maybe there wasn't any good football on the night before Thanksgiving. The people in the bar seemed into it.

Except—yes, there he was, at a corner table over by the kitchen door, Mal Umbertini, dressed in turquoise, staring at Evan through the boisterous crowd.

Evan threaded his way to Mal's tiny table. Mal kicked a chair out, and Evan squeezed into it, his knees bumping Mal's.

"Hi." He had to lean in to Mal's personal space in order to be heard over the crowd and the music. His heart was thumping.

"Doyle," said Mal.

"Umbertini."

"Caro must have told you about my new favorite bar."

"Yeah," drawled Evan, squinting at the big-screen TVs. "I'm kind of surprised."

"It's a change."

"I guess."

A waitress materialized—Even though this place was hopping, the service seemed to be excellent. Possibly because the waitress and Mal were friends. They exchanged significant glances while Mal ordered a pint of beer for Evan. She gave him a cool stare, one eyebrow raised, and whisked away, ponytail swinging.

"Yikes," said Evan. "I hope she doesn't spit in my glass."

"I wouldn't put it past her."

"Jealous girlfriend?" Evan teased.

"You know better than that," said Mal, one corner of his mouth curling up in a smile.

"Uh, the guys in this bar, have they ever—"

"Nah, I haven't had any problem," said Mal, still smiling. "I thought they seemed a bit Stormtrooper-esque at first too, but honestly they really just seem to care about sports."

Evan's heart was still banging in his chest. It felt a little like fear, but it wasn't—he was wildly excited just to be near Mal again. Mal looked beautiful in a linen sports coat over an open-throated aqua shirt. And hot, and his eyes were warm. Mal was smiling at him, and Evan was so fucking happy to see him, he was nearly trembling with it.

"So I wanted to tell you." He strove to keep an even tone. "The kneecap is called a patella. Not a patera. I don't know what a patera zone is."

"Oh, damn," said Mal. "That seemed like such a cool name for a sports bar. Sort of macabre and ironic, like calling a swimming pool the Ear Infection Place."

"Sure. Because this bar is clearly so macabre and ironic."

Mal laughed. In the dim light of the bar, his eyes were dark as ebony, gleaming with golden light under devilish brows.

Evan couldn't stop smiling.

The waitress swept imperiously past and plunked Evan's beer down in front of him, sharply enough that some slopped over the top. He mopped the table with a napkin, then drank. In his nervousness, he downed half of the beer right away. "Caroline is scared that it'll be awkward tomorrow."

"Yes, she's been working on me too," said Mal. "Thanksgiving is very important to her."

"To you too," said Evan. "I'm the one who's kind of invading your yearly ritual."

"Oh, no," said Mal. "That's not true. It was always her day for remembering, you know. It was on a Thanksgiving that she first told me all about you." He sipped his beer. "What do you do on Thanksgiving? I mean, until now."

"I go camping." Mal pulled an appalled face, and Evan grinned. "You don't camp?"

"Not in that sense, no," said Mal. "I guess I probably slept in a tent in the backyard at some point, with my cousins. Not lately."

Evan tried to picture Mal roughing it. The mental image was incongruous, to say the least. "It's sort of good to get lost," he said. "I used to go sleep on the beach, in the dunes south of San Diego. Nobody around for miles and miles. Just stars and wind."

"And dirt. Bugs. Scorpions?"

"Uh-huh," agreed Evan.

"Snakes."

"Sure. All those beach snakes." He sipped his beer. "Last Thanksgiving was my first one in Oregon. I tried to do the same thing on the beach here, but it rained so hard I was scared I'd literally get washed out to sea. I ended up in a motel in Newport."

"Camping sounds like so much fun," said Mal dryly. The waitress blew past, and Mal called, "Oh, Sherman?" She paused. "What's a patera?"

Her eyes widened. "Seahawks coach Jack Patera?" she said, like she was explaining the color of the sky.

"Oh," said Mal, innocently. "Was he a good coach?"

"Legendary! And he was an Oregonian, you know."

Then she was gone again, and Mal said to Evan, "That is so disappointing."

"I know."

"My idea was better."

"You could open your own competing sports bar," suggested Evan, "called the Patella Zone. To celebrate kneecap injuries."

Mal's eyes widened. "An injury-themed sports bar?"

"A sports-injury bar."

"It could be decorated with big posters of famous football accidents. Guys rolling on the ground clutching their legs."

"Even better," Evan said, "I bet you could stream montages on these big TVs of athletes getting hurt through history."

"Holy shit, Evan, that is such a good idea. Is there enough footage to do that?"

"Oh, God, there has to be. Maybe not if you're just looking at football. But if you included the Olympics? Definitely. And rodeos and whatever. Soccer."

Mal's brow wrinkled. "Do people get hurt playing soccer?"

"I mean, I've never watched soccer in my life," admitted Evan. "But do you remember when there was a big scandal, a few years ago, when one soccer player bit someone?"

Mal laughed again—he had a light, unexpected almost-giggle when something tickled him. "That seems unsportsmanlike."

"Yeah, people were really mad. It was on the news."

"We're going to be millionaires," said Mal. "We'll quit our jobs and open a bar that uses cold beer and nonstop slo-mo biting videos to celebrate the impermanence of victory and the fragility of the human body."

"The Patella Zone," said Evan, raising his glass. "Where things can go horribly wrong at any moment."

They clinked their glasses together, both now laughing. Then Mal's eyes, shining with mirth, met Evan's, and his laughter died as he drew in a breath.

The current of attraction was flowing between them, strong as ever, strong as a shot of vodka. The blood rushed out of Evan's brain and into his groin, and a reckless impulse took hold of him.

Oh, hell. It was a terrible idea, the worst idea, but he didn't care. He'd be miserable later. Right now he wanted sex with Mal. Tonight. He could have Mal's skin, his sweat, his mouth, his dick. Now.

Mal met his eyes, and his pupils dilated.

Evan drained his beer, set the glass down with a *crack*. "Ready to go?"

They spilled out of the Patera Zone and onto the street, dizzy and drunk on excitement and happiness as much as beer. They walked fast, hand in hand, toward Mal's town house, threading through other pedestrians on the sidewalk. At some point someone jostled them, and Mal stumbled into Evan, who grabbed him by the lapels and dragged his face down for a kiss. Whoever they'd run into laughed and said, "*They're* in a hurry." Mal put his hands behind his own back, and they spun on the sidewalk, kissing, exhilarated, Evan's hands in Mal's hair.

They went past Evan's truck, where Dulcie sat alertly in the passenger seat, ears cocked. "You should get the dog," said Mal.

"She can stay in the truck," breathed Evan, towing Mal toward the town house. "This won't take long."

Mal slowed, braced his feet against Evan's pull. "It could," he urged. "You could stay a while. Get the dog."

Evan didn't want to wait. He slid his arms around Mal, fingers threaded through his at the small of his back, and then pulled his long beautiful body against his own. He was already hard, breathing fast against Mal's neck. He whispered, "Come on, hurry," and felt Mal shiver.

They were now at Mal's doorstep. Evan trotted up the stairs to Mal's door.

"Don't," Mal said softly.

Evan glanced back over his shoulder. Mal wasn't behind him—he was still down on the sidewalk, lit by the streetlight. His hands still behind his back, his hair rumpled.

"What?"

"Don't, Evan. Please."

"Don't what?" Evan came back down the stairs. He stood on the bottom step, where he was taller than Mal, and put his hands on Mal's shoulders, drawing him in.

Mal tilted his head back to look up at him, throat exposed. "Please don't jerk me around."

Evan's face went hot, dismay piercing his fog of lust. He dropped his hands from Mal's shoulders. "I—I didn't mean to. I'm sorry. I just— I missed—"

Mal looked the same as always, handsome, sardonic, and a little remote. But his eyes were intense, burning with emotion.

You know him well enough to not pay attention to his face, right?

"You called it, Evan." Mal's voice was low, vibrating with passion. "I was full of shit when I said I could be your fuck buddy. I want more than twelve minutes of your time tonight. And tomorrow night too. I want *time* with you. I want breakfast with you after you've spent the night in bed with me. I want you to invite me to your place. I want to *date*."

Evan's face tingled with the fierceness of his blush. Mal moved in closer. "I want to tell my mom about you. I want to take you to the goddamn office holiday party and introduce you to my colleagues as my boyfriend. I want to buy Dulcie a dog bed for my house. I want to give you half my closet for your stuff."

Really?

Evan swallowed against the lump of fear in his throat, then wrapped his arms around Mal's shoulders, pulled him in for a hug. It wasn't sexual, really, not this time.

Mal's cheek was against Evan's, his voice in his ear. "Evan. You look *horrified*. I'm sorry. I just— You say 'I'm done' one week and 'Let's go' tonight, and I'm all for it, sweetheart. Whatever you want. But I can't pretend— I don't want to pretend that it's nothing to me. I'll do whatever you want, but that's because I'm all in. Not because it's not important."

It was exactly how Evan felt too. He squeezed Mal tight. "I'm not horrified," he managed to say.

What if it were true? What if Mal really wanted to be with him? What if Evan had hurt him?

What if he, Evan, had a little courage? A little faith. This once.

"I," he stammered. "I— Mal, could we talk? Just talk?"

They went into the town house, and Evan didn't let him turn on any lights, but pushed him through the foyer and onto the couch. He climbed on top of Mal, straddled him. "I'm sorry," he said, into Mal's hair. "I'm a huge asshole. I didn't mean to be. Caroline told me you felt like that and I didn't believe her."

"I told you how I felt," said Mal, whose hands were down by his sides on the sofa cushions, but whose face was turned into Evan's neck.

"I didn't believe you, either." Evan rubbed his palms in circles on his back, his own heart beating painfully in his chest. "I barely believe it now. I'm sorry," he said again. "I don't know how to do this."

He closed his eyes, pressed his forehead to Mal's shoulder.

They'd never done this. He'd come over to this town house lots of times, but never to talk. *Grow up. Just talk.*

"Tell me what you're thinking," said Mal, in his ear.

Evan rested his chin on Mal's shoulder, aware that he was hiding his face. "Years of therapy," he said. "But zero role models for healthy relationships, like none. And I'm, oh God, Mal. I've been told so many times, and I know it's true, that I'm not broken, or guilty or wrong, or too fucked up for a normal life. But I still feel like you, someone like you, can't really want me."

"What's a someone like me?" murmured Mal, leaning into Evan.

"Someone straight," said Evan. Mal huffed against his neck, and Evan added, "Not straight like the opposite of gay. Straight like the opposite of *crooked*."

"You're beautiful."

Evan shivered.

"You're perfect. Inside and out, Evan."

"I— I'm— I can't. We— If we were going to date. If we were going to be together, really together. We would need to talk about the sex. I'm really, really—"

"Easy." Mal shushed him, and Evan steadied himself by burrowing into Mal's body, legs tight around his hips, arms around his shoulders. Like a drowning man clinging to a floating spar. Determined to get through this conversation if it killed him.

Mal, his voice a soothing murmur, said, "If you're worried about the whole top/bottom thing, you have to know that I absolutely do not care if we never do it. I'm dead serious. It can be blowjobs forever."

Evan breathed, "I think about it, though."

"What?"

"Sex. Fucking. I want to. All the time."

Mal shuddered. He pressed his face to Evan's neck, and his voice was throaty when he said, "I'm *such* a jackass. So do I."

"You do? With me?"

Mal laughed. "Yes."

Evan closed his eyes tight, squeezed Mal hard enough to press the breath out of his lungs. "Boyfriend?"

"Yeah," said Mal, short-winded. "Your jackass boyfriend."

"You don't know what you're getting into, though. I have to tell you— Oh, I do need the dog for this. Hang on." Evan climbed off his lap, stumbled to the door. "Stay there. I'll be right back."

He went out to his truck and fetched Dulcie. She was *delighted* to be back in Mal's town house. She danced around, ears flattened and entire body wagging, her toenails clicking on the laminate floor, then crowded against Mal's shins and rested her head on his knee.

"I'm so flattered," Mal said, petting her. "I'm happy to see you too."

"That's the nice thing about a dog," said Evan, kicking off his shoes and sitting on the couch next to Mal. "She shows you just how she feels, all the time."

They both petted her, Mal fondling her ears, Evan scratching her neck. Their fingers brushed together. "You're like that too," said Mal. "It's one of the things I like about you."

"Yeah, right."

"Hey, stop rejecting my compliments. I'm serious."

"Oh." Evan turned so he was kneeling on the couch, facing Mal. He leaned into him, one hand on Mal's arm, the other on Dulcie's head. "Okay," he said, his face close to Mal's neck, where his face couldn't be seen. "I'm going to tell you something horrible. Listen. Listen to me."

He felt Mal nod.

"Thanksgiving. I was sixteen. Nez took me. He put me in the back of the truck and drove away. I was in a weird daze. Mom— I had— I told you what I'd just done."

"Yeah."

"Yes. So. I was, like. 'This is not the real world and none of this is really happening,' so when Nez put me in the back of his truck and drove away, I just—I just went."

"People sometimes dissociate during trauma," said Mal. "It's not unusual."

"I know. So Nez eventually pulled over, on the road from Barstow to El Centro. It's the Mojave desert. Middle of the night, no cars for miles and miles. He—he raped me in the back of the truck, and he made me . . . he made me—"

"Evan," said Mal, his voice soft. "This doesn't matter."

"He made me come like a racehorse." He felt the gasp in Mal's body. "I know, right? What do you *do* with that piece of information?"

"It—it still doesn't matter." Mal's voice sounded a little strained. "It was just your body's reaction. It didn't—"

"I *know*." Evan pressed closer to Mal, hand wrapped tightly around his bicep. Dulcie licked his wrist. "He liked that—he said it was because I wanted it so bad—but that was a lie. It wasn't consent. It was an involuntary physiological response. I know that. But I didn't know it *then*, Mal, do you see? And I was . . ." Evan closed his eyes and remembered the annihilating blackness of his despair. "I was so ashamed."

"Sweetheart."

"It was so bad. I can't tell you," he said. "And also— I only—
Before that I only went to the En with Derrick for a few months. Like,
it was hardly anything. I've met people who turned tricks for *years* and
they're fine, they can shake it off. I blew, like, twelve guys, and I wasn't
fine. And then Mom died, and then Nez raped me, and I— And it all
sort of seemed like something I deserved, because—"

"No," said Mal sharply.

"No." Evan breathed. "I know. I do."

He pulled back a little and let Mal see his face. The room was dim,
Mal's eyes black, shadowed by his heavy brows.

Evan kept going—he had to get it all out. "So. When I was with
Nez. At first, I submitted to him. Sort of like I was trying to show
him that I was a good kid, so he wouldn't hurt me. But I know that
doesn't mean I consented. And that when I—when I responded,
that doesn't mean I consented either. So that's how it was, the first,
um, the first few times. But once he got me set up in the house in El
Centro, in his room with a bolt on the outside of the door, and I was
like, 'Oh, I get it, this is going to be my whole *life* now.' I stopped
eating then, and started fighting, every time. I fought as hard as I
could, I made him beat me up, I made him bind me, so that— I don't
get off on that at all, so that— Maybe I was trying to get him to kill
me, because I tried to escape and couldn't, and I— Anyway.

"But then the cops came, and got me out, and I got help. I
had foster parents who took care of me, took me to therapy, and
I got help. And I haven't felt like that—that shame, in a long time.
Okay, Mal? I need you to know that I'm a lot better. I'm not that
boy anymore. I'm pretty strong." He dared a glance at Mal. "I know
I'm not broken. I know I don't have anything to be ashamed of. But
still, that shame. I can't explain how bad it hurts, to be ashamed like
that. It hurts like a physical pain that just doesn't stop. Sometimes,
I would have just—I would have stopped existing, just from hating
myself so much, from so much shame—"

Mal was shaking his head mutely.

"But I didn't," said Evan. "I know the shame is a lie. But I'm afraid
of it, afraid I'll go back there. Do you see?"

"Evan." Mal leaned his head forward so that his forehead touched
Evan's, his eyes closed. "This is appalling. I don't know what to say."
His voice was a whisper. "Tell me what you need me to say."

"I need you to understand that it isn't rational." Evan rested his cheek on Mal's warm shoulder. "I'm not always rational, and I know that, but it's an ongoing thing you would have to deal with. I know that having sex with you would never be like rape, Mal. Or like the En. I know that. Of course I know it. But like . . . when Caroline surprised me on the street, and I panicked. Even though I know Caroline would never hurt me. You surprised me before, when I was feeling vulnerable and weird, and I panicked. It's not rational. It's stress from trauma, and it's turned into a disorder, and now I spend my life avoiding things that make me think I'll feel like that again."

"Like me?"

Mal's body was turned toward him, and Evan was curled into the shelter of him. Evan slid his palms over his shoulders, cradled his head.

"It's not about you. Sometimes I'll feel bad, and sometimes I'll feel fine, and it won't be anything you did or anything you could have fixed. I'm a fucked-up mess sometimes."

"Everyone's a fucked-up mess sometimes." Mal's eyes were shining, golden brown, beautiful. "I'm a sarcastic jerk sometimes. We can . . . we could go to therapy together, if you want. If you think it'll help."

"We could? Have you ever gone to therapy?"

"No."

"How come?"

"Because the thought of talking about my emotions to a stranger makes me feel ill." Mal grimaced. "Really, it doesn't appeal. But I don't want to lose you, either, because I said or did the wrong thing without meaning to. So, yeah. I would. If you want to."

Oh, Mal. Evan's heart ached with admiration in that moment. Mal had been hurt so bad before, and he'd always dealt with it on his own terms. But he was ready to try a different way, for Evan.

For that matter, considering he'd once found his lover's body and had been kicked out by his parents, Mal probably needed therapy as much as Evan did. Maybe more.

He needed something else too.

"Look," Evan said.

He took off his watch and unbuckled his leather bracelet, then held up his hands, palms down. "I want you to see this. It's not bad." He rotated his arms, displaying the way the scars entirely encircled his wrists, thicker over the knobby bones, almost invisible across the tender white skin at base of his hand.

Mal's dark head bent over Evan's wrists. "I see," he said softly, examining the white, shining scars.

"It's from the zip ties," Evan said. "I didn't do it. I've never tried to kill myself. I wanted to disappear, sometimes, but I never thought about how or when I would do it. And I don't want to do that anymore. I don't think that way now."

Mal kissed Evan's wrists, a brush of his lips. "Will you . . . will you do something for me?" he whispered.

"What?"

"Promise me. If you feel that blackness again, you'll talk to someone. Me, or Caro, or go to therapy, or call a fucking hotline or something. Even if we're not together, not anything, just— I want—I want you to stay."

"I promise," agreed Evan. He'd already made that promise to himself.

"Yeah?"

"Yes. Yes to everything. I wanna try. To be your boyfriend, I mean. I don't know if I can. I don't know if you still want to, after hearing all that. God, Mal. I could go, and no hard feelings, okay? But do you still think you want to be my—my jackass boyfriend?"

"I want to," said Mal, immediately. "Oh, yes, Evan, please."

Okay. A surge of mingled happiness and terror surged through him. They were going to do this. A relationship.

We should seal the deal with sex. Wasn't that what boyfriends would do?

Evan began to open Mal's shirt, and was surprised by how much trouble he had with the buttons. Mal murmured, "What are you—" but Evan cut him off with a kiss. He crawled into his lap, pressing against him, still fumbling with the buttons, tearing one.

Mal pulled away and surged up, using his body to dump Evan onto his back on the couch. "What are you doing?" he asked. "You want sex *now*?"

"Yes?" Evan's voice broke. "Don't you?"

"No!" Mal sounded appalled. "Sweetheart, you're *shivering*. Your nerves are all wound up. I cannot have sex with you when you're like this. This is not my scene."

Oh. Was he unattractive now? Was Mal going to see a scared brutalized kid whenever he looked at Evan?

But Mal leaned down, his face inches from Evan's, his breath warm against his lips. "I always want you," he murmured. "Always, always. But I only do it if it's fun. I don't do it to prove a point or whatever is happening right now."

Evan nodded. His teeth were chattering with nerves.

"We are not just about sex, you and me," whispered Mal, and then kissed him on the forehead. "And I only do it when it's fun. Why don't you stay here and pet Dulcie for a minute? I'm going to get us some water and a snack. Okay?"

Evan nodded again.

Mal kissed him, his mouth soft. "Be right back."

CHAPTER FIFTEEN

They ate cheese and crackers and shared a tall glass of ice water, sitting shoulder to shoulder on the couch. After several minutes of companionable silence, Evan felt his body unwind.

Dulcie was tranquil too, sprawled on her back, belly exposed and folded paws in the air, and Evan rubbed her chest with his foot.

"Does Dulcie like cheese?" asked Mal.

"Dulcie loves cheese," Evan said. "She knows she's not supposed to beg for treats, but I promise you she's thinking about cheese right now."

"Can I give her some?"

"Best not to. Unless you make her do a trick or something first. Then it's not begging; it's a reward."

"Like what?"

"Dulcie," said Evan, in a pay-attention tone. Dulcie immediately flipped onto her feet. "Go to bed." She trotted to the kitchen and lay down on the rug there. "Dulcie, come." She came back. "Sit." She sat, eyes shining with hope. Evan smiled at her. "Good girl. Now you get some cheese."

"What a rigmarole," said Mal, feeding her a morsel.

"Nah, it's good," said Evan. "She's a very serious little person, you know. She has a lot of responsibility. But she's only six. It comforts her to know exactly what she's supposed to be doing and why things are happening."

"Hm. Me too." They sat amicably for a moment, passing the glass of water back and forth. "Hey, Evan? Remember when you said the hands thing was a hard rule? Do you think it always will be? Because I would like to touch you. Sometimes. I could wait, though. I could wait for you to be ready."

Evan felt a renewed stab of anxiety. "I'm sorry. I don't think I'm ever going to want to let you grab my dick."

Mal widened his eyes. "No, no. That's fine. You've got a right to tell me to not grab your dick. I meant . . . I'd like to touch your shoulder and hold hands and things like that. I don't want to make you uncomfortable, but I do want to be affectionate sometimes."

"Oh." Evan smiled at him. "Well. Yeah, we could work on that."

"Really?" Mal's face cleared and his eyes lit up. "Yeah?"

"Yeah."

"I want to be clear that you can give *me* a handy anytime you want."

Evan laughed. "I'll keep that in mind. Want to touch my shoulder?"

Mal nodded.

"Okay."

Mal carefully put down the glass of water, then sat back beside Evan and ran a palm over his bicep and the ball of his shoulder. "Okay?"

"Yeah." He leaned into Mal's hand. Mal traced a thumb along his collarbone, squeezed his trapezius, and Evan huffed with pleasure. "Feels good."

"Feels good to me, too," murmured Mal. "I like your shoulders." And he kissed him.

They kissed for a while, unhurried. Mal explored his mouth, playfully flicking his tongue against Evan's, nibbling on his lips. All the while, his hand stroked Evan's shoulder. Nothing about it felt hurried, and Evan relaxed into it, humming.

Then Mal broke the kiss to ask, "Want a backrub?"

Evan's body buzzed with arousal. He nuzzled kisses against Mal's jaw, relishing the rasp of stubble against his lips and tongue. "Hmm?"

Mal pulled back, and Evan blinked his eyes open. Mal's lips were red. He bit one, and there was indecision and hope in his expression. "My hands, your shoulders and back. Maybe your neck, if it's okay with you. That's all."

Mal's hand on his shoulder felt nice, and Evan hadn't had a backrub in years. "Back, shoulders, and neck," he agreed, knowing that he sounded cagy. "Don't grab. Don't pin me down. Don't go below the belt. Don't reach around."

"I won't."

"I'm serious."

"I will never do any of that, not ever, unless you tell me I can. I promise. Backrub only. Or not, if you don't want to."

And he found that he trusted Mal. He had always known that Mal wouldn't deliberately hurt him. He just needed to be brave. "Okay."

Mal smiled at him, full lips curving. "Yeah?"

"Yeah."

"Let's go upstairs."

Ten minutes later he was shirtless and gleaming with oil in Mal's bed, melting like butter into the mattress. Almost drooling with pleasure, more relaxed than he'd been in—ever.

This was a good idea.

"I lived with a chiropractor for about a year." Mal was sitting astride Evan's ass, his warm hands caressing down Evan's spine. "He was a jerk. But he did teach me how to give a good massage."

"Mm."

"You keep a lot of tension right *here*," murmured Mal, talented fingers easing more almond oil into the knots of muscles in the small of Evan's back, producing a mix of pain and pleasure that nearly brought tears to Evan's eyes. "Do you get backaches?"

Evan hummed affirmatively.

"Headaches?"

"Mm-hmm."

Mal massaged up Evan's body, until his fingertips found something tight, just at the base of Evan's skull. "There's your headaches, sweetheart, right there."

Evan whimpered with pleasure as tension he hadn't even known was there was eased. He was nearly entranced now, but his dick was engorged and hard, bent sideways in his jeans and sandwiched between his abdomen and the bed. Mal was turned on too—Evan could tell by his breathing and his smell—but his hands never strayed from their task, and though he straddled Evan's butt, he didn't intrude upon it. Strictly professional.

After a while, Evan decided to do something about that. "Let me up." Mal lifted off him so he could turn over onto his back. Evan adjusted his dick in his jeans, grunting. When Mal's eyes dropped to watch him do it, Evan grinned up at him. "Want me to do you?"

"Sure."

"I mean," he added, awkwardly, "not *do* you do you. I mean rub your back."

Mal laughed, a happy gurgle in his throat. "That too."

So Mal took off his shirt and spread himself out on the bed, and Evan sat on his thighs, warmed some of the almond oil in his palms, and smoothed it over his back. "A chiropractor, huh?" he murmured. *Mine*, he thought, tracing Mal's scapulae.

"Yep."

This skin, warm and brown and dotted here and there with moles, was his to touch, no one else's. He smiled at himself. It was new, this possessiveness. He isolated the muscles at the back of Mal's neck and said, pedantically, "This is the trapezius." He massaged the muscles and felt Mal relax. "Here are your deltoids. Levator scapulae is under *here* somewhere," he added, digging in with his thumbs.

"Umm," murmured Mal. "He didn't tell me the fancy Latin names."

"He was a chiropractor. He probably didn't know them."

"Bitchy."

Evan was smiling, stroking Mal's body and grinding his groin into Mal's butt through their clothes. Unlike Mal's unimpeachably professional massage, Evan was not pretending this was anything but foreplay. "Infraspinatus. Teres major."

"I'm definitely going to challenge you to show up my ex-boyfriends more often."

"Latissimus dorsi. External abdominal oblique." Mal snickered, and Evan's fingers teased. "Ticklish?"

Mal squirmed. "Stop!"

Evan braced his hands on the bed and leaned forward to kiss the back of Mal's neck, his mouth open and tasting, his erection lodged between Mal's lean buns. "Are we having fun yet?"

"I am," said Mal breathlessly.

Evan lasciviously licked the side of his neck, rocking his hips. "Sternocleidomastoid," he purred, and felt Mal's body pulse with laughter. "Do you ever bottom?" he asked, his dick throbbing as he continued to grind it between Mal's glutei maximi.

"Sure, if you want." Mal reached out and grasped the slats of his headboard and began to rock in time with Evan's thrusts. Evan's breath shortened, his pleasure climbing.

"Yeah, but do you like to, ever?"

"Hmm, my butt's not really very sexy."

"Oh, I dunno." Evan snorted in his ear, and felt Mal laugh once more.

"Thank you, but I mean it's not very erogenous. It just doesn't seem to be wired that way, it doesn't excite me."

"My nipples are like that," Evan admitted, kissing Mal's trapezius again. "Nothing going on there." He slid a hand under Mal's body across his pectorals, found Mal's pointed nipples. "Not like yours," he murmured, pinching gently.

Mal growled softly, arching his back. "I'll do it if you want. If it's turning you on, that'll get me going. Want to?"

"I never have." Evan's body was covering Mal's now, and he was enjoying the feel of him beneath him, fragrant and warm. Even more enjoyable was imagining Mal doing this to *him*. The bed began to creak as their movements increased. "Are you getting off on the mattress, Mal?" he whispered.

"Almost," muttered Mal.

"Would a blowjob be fun?"

"Oh yeah." He rolled over, lifted his hips off the bed so that Evan could strip off his pants. His cock bounced tautly against his abdomen; it was dark red-brown and slick. "Sixty-nine would be even more fun."

"Would it?" Another thing Evan had never trusted anyone enough to try. "Okay." He swiftly got naked and arranged himself on his side of the bed, aligning his own junk with Mal's face and getting an intimate view of Mal's.

"Want a condom?" offered Mal.

"I—" Mal had blown him bare before, and it had felt amazing, but now he found himself wanting the barrier. "I always use one. I don't need it, but I— Is that okay?"

"Okay with me." He stretched for his bedside table, and handed a foil square to Evan. "Okay if I don't?"

"Yeah," whispered Evan, rolling the condom onto himself.

Mal's cock quivered alertly, and Evan wrapped an arm around Mal's hips and licked the hot tender skin covering his shaft. This was the first uncovered cock he'd had in his mouth since he was much younger. Mal tasted a little sweaty. Better than the condom. Evan frenched sloppy kisses down the shaft, giving it lots of drool, suckling the corpus spongiosum, reveling in Mal's gasp. Then Mal's mouth engulfed his own erection, hot and wet, and he grunted.

Side by side they lay on the bed. Mal's cock was a pleasure to have in his mouth: salty and velvety and rigid, plenty long but not too thick, with a smooth flared head, juicy with pre-come. It slid smoothly through his mouth, into his throat. But what Mal was doing to Evan's dick was a distraction that he was incapable of ignoring. Evan gave it his best try, but proved to be a lousy multitasker; the pleasure got so intense, so fast, he couldn't concentrate, couldn't breathe or think. He released Mal from his mouth and buried his face in the mattress, moaning, "Sorry, I'm sorry."

Mal hastily spat him out. "What? Should I stop?"

"No no *no*, don't stop," gasped Evan. "Don't st— Oh God, yes, thank you, oh my God." He tightened his hand on his base and Mal got a little rough with him, sucking hard, using his teeth. "*Yeah*," panted Evan. "Do *that*. Oh, more. Yeah, oh Mal, oh—" He pressed his face against Mal's thigh as joy rose up in him, so sweet and so fast. "Fuck, *yes*," he groaned, and came in a long exquisite rush, and Mal sucked him through the spasms until he flinched away.

When, after a long moment, he could breathe again, he turned and grabbed Mal by the hips. Now that Mal wasn't short-circuiting his brain, he remembered just what Mal liked. He knew exactly how to tease him and drive him wild and make him scream.

So he did.

In the steaming aftermath, he lapped creamy spunk from Mal's belly, the crisp hair there tickling his tongue. Mal's semen tasted a little musky, a little like chlorine. Not bad at all.

Nuzzling, Evan said, "I don't think I'm too good at sixty-nine."

"Are you kidding?" said Mal, his voice deep and drowsy. "That made me feel like an amazing sex superhero."

A smile of pure happiness stretched across Evan's face. He cuddled against Mal's side. "I like your come noises," he said. "You always sound so surprised. Like, 'Oh, what's happening to me?'"

"*Pleasantly* surprised," murmured Mal, around a yawn. "Like, 'Oh, I am so in love with you, and look, there you are, sucking my dick.'"

Evan's eyes snapped open.

He tried to say *I love you too*. Which was, after all, entirely true. But what came out was a stammered, "I guess that would be a pleasant surprise."

Mal laughed through his nose, an undignified snort of slightly bitter amusement, and Evan curled on his side, away from Mal, wrapping his arms around his head. "Shit, I'm sorry," he said. "I'm so stupid. That came out so bad."

"It's okay." Mal was still laughing.

"I, no, I—"

"Don't, sweetheart," said Mal soothingly. "You don't have to say anything. I shouldn't have blurted that out. I was halfway asleep."

But I love you, I want you to know that I do.

The moment had passed, though. If he said it now, Mal wouldn't believe him. Would think he was just saying it.

Suddenly Evan was tired, not just relaxed but worn thin. Because even when things were going great, like tonight, he still managed to make mistakes. How often would he accidentally hurt Mal's feelings? How often would Mal let him, before he got tired of it?

He sat up. "What time is it? I should go home."

"Almost midnight." Mal was watching him. Observant Mal. He clearly knew that Evan was struggling with something. His voice was neutral as he said, "Tomorrow's Thanksgiving—we both have Thursday and Friday off, right? Why don't you just go to sleep? I have a toothbrush you can borrow. Go home in the morning to change, and I'll meet you at Caro's place in the afternoon."

Evan eyed him, considering. He wanted to say yes—to say yes to his boyfriend—but his chest felt tight with anxiety. "Thanks, but . . . I think tonight I'm gonna go. I— This was awesome, but it was a lot. I think I need to sleep in my normal place."

"Okay."

Had that been too easy? What was Mal really thinking? And oh God, how was he going to get through *Thanksgiving*?

Evan tried to match Mal's calm though. "I'll see you at Kiki's tomorrow for enchiladas. And after—after, do you want to come up to my house? For the night?"

Mal gazed at him. Evan let him look into his face, his nervous, hopeful eyes.

Mal smiled. "I'd like that."

CHAPTER SIXTEEN

Thanksgiving at Caro's was a little weird.

"Happy Thanksgiving," said Mal, greeting Evan at the door to Caro's cottage and angling in for a kiss.

Evan stepped backward, bringing the bakery pie he'd brought up between them like a shield. "Hey." He was smiling, but it was taut. "Hi."

Mal backed down. "Hi to you too. Everything okay?"

"Sure. Is Kiki here?" Evan edged inside, not touching Mal.

After yesterday's intense conversation, playful sex, and swift withdrawal, Mal had hoped for a little more warmth. But blurting out *I love you* like it was a bit of playful banter clearly had been a serious miscalculation. All of Evan's happy sexy ease had vanished; his spark had died before Mal's eyes like a blown-out birthday candle. And then Evan himself had hit the bricks. There and gone, just like that. Just like before.

That was how Thanksgiving went. Evan was funny, friendly, and—was Mal imagining it?—distant. He mostly kept his eyes on his sister, and didn't touch Mal, or flirt with him, or exchange sexy glances with him.

Patience, Mal schooled his heart.

Not that it was a disaster. He'd always loved the ritual of spending this day with Caro, and, as always, the food was an adventure. Caro's homemade enchiladas fell apart into a sort of soupy slop. They were spicy and delicious beneath their layer of bubbly melted cheese, but they were definitely more liquid than enchiladas were supposed to be. Caro rechristened the dish Enchilada Dip, and they scooped up the mess with tortilla chips. It was good.

The movies were good too—Caro had lined up a roster of black-and-whites with her favorite leading men, which meant a lot of Cary Grant. A lot.

"I think that's very queer indeed," said Mary Nash, in her role as Katharine Hepburn's upper-class mother in *The Philadelphia Story*, and Evan smiled.

"She reminds me of your mom," he said to Mal.

"Oh, please don't buy Mom's Main Line old-money act," said Mal. "Her family had high WASP pretentions, but by the time she was born they were flat broke. Her dad was the kind of guy who would reminisce about his college days at New Haven, and just let people assume he went to Yale, not Southern Connecticut State. Her mother served eggs poached in oatmeal for dinner for weeks at a time, because he drank his paycheck every month and they couldn't afford anything else."

"Reasonably nutritious," said Caro, crunching on a chip, "but gross."

"Yeah, that would get real old," said Evan. "Dorothy still won't touch oatmeal."

"They *loathed* my dad, who was Catholic and slightly off-white," continued Mal, adorning a tortilla chip with a dollop of guacamole.

"Italian is off-white?" asked Evan.

"To my mom's people, yes. But what they hated most was that he earned a lot of money. His money was so clean and new that it reeked of shame."

"What did he do?"

"Umbertini Chevrolet," said Mal. "Three convenient locations to serve you in Prince Frederick, Dunkirk, Upper Marlboro. Mom's parents never forgave Mom for marrying him. One of my dad's wedding presents to her was to pay off their mortgage for them. They never forgave him for that, either."

"I don't even understand what you're saying," admitted Evan. "Old money, new? If you own your house and have a college degree, who cares? What's the difference? I guess money comes with its own, like, secret language. If you never had any, you never learn it."

Mal shrugged. "It's not about money really; it's this whole weird culture of East Coast prep-school bullshit. They couldn't afford the lifestyle, but they didn't want anyone to know that. They'd say things like, 'We *used* to summer in Maine, but it's gotten so humid, and the boat's just temporarily in dry dock for repairs.' I had to leave home before I realized how few people give a shit."

"Our mom worked in a grocery store," said Evan, "and our dad was a name on a piece of paper."

Caro dimpled. "We used to pretend he was a Russian spy."

"Well, he had the best name for it." They both laughed. "Remember when we went to the library to look up 'Farkas'?"

"We were about thirteen," said Caro, including Mal in the story with a glance. "That was the day we realized that dad wasn't a Russian spy—he was just a lying asshole."

"It means 'wolf,' right?" said Mal.

"Yep," said Evan. "Wolfgang Farkas. Wolf Wolf. The man gave our mom a fantasy novel alias before impregnating her and vanishing."

Caro was grinning. "I sort of imagine that Wolfgang Farkas was his favorite *Dungeons and Dragons* character's name."

"I used to lurk around Society for Creative Anachronism websites," said Evan, "thinking maybe I'd find Wolfgang Farkas was there, making chain mail out of beer tabs, or showing off his mad crossbow skills."

"Find him?"

"Nah. Not sure what I'd have done if I did."

Caro nudged Evan. "I was reading the Harry Potter books a few years ago—have you read them?—and there's a werewolf character named Remus Lupin. I so wished I could call you, Alex, and say, 'Guess what! I've found Dad's middle name! Wolfgang Lupin Farkas.'"

"Wolf Wolf Wolf."

"They call him El Lobo."

"He also told her he was in the Navy."

"He probably said he was in love with the sea."

"Sorry, baby, El Lobo mates for life."

They collapsed in giggles.

Mal watched them laugh, knowing that his own smile was a bit twisted.

Their childhood had been infinitely worse than Mal's. His dad had been a homophobe, yes, but he'd been present at the dinner table every night of Mal's life. He'd gruffly made sure Mal completed all his homework. Provided the basics: food, shelter, safety. A means of escape, even: Mal had gotten a car for his sixteenth birthday. Evan, at sixteen, had faced the unimaginable dilemma of how to protect his sister from a predatory adult lifestyle that had already consumed his mother. And while Mal had been sulking in his room about how poorly understood he was, Caro and Evan had been rationing food. Yet there was little bitterness in their laughter.

Trying to speak lightly, he said, "How come I'm over here grinding my teeth about my jerk family, and you two are laughing?"

"Well," said Caro, kindly, "you were on your own. We had each other."

After dinner, Caro went to the kitchen to dish up Evan's key lime pie, and Mal and Evan followed her there; they all ended up standing around the kitchen, eating pie and arguing about which movie to watch next. Then Evan said, "I'm going to take the dog around the block."

"Want company?" asked Mal, hoping for a chance to talk to him alone.

"No, it's fine," said Evan, putting on his shoes. "I'll be right back."

He clicked his tongue for Dulcie, and they vanished out the kitchen door into the backyard. Mal watched him wistfully.

"Cary Grant or Jimmy Stewart?" Caro asked.

"Grant."

"Correct."

"Cary Grant or Gary Cooper?" he ventured.

"Grant."

He shook his head. "I disagree. Cooper. Young Cooper."

"Young Cooper over young Grant?"

"Admittedly it's a tough call."

"Not for me. Young Cooper or Clark Gable?"

"*Argh*. Gable. Right? Gable looks like he'd be up for *anything*."

"I'd take Cary Grant over either of them."

"You have a loyal heart."

She nudged him with her foot, gestured with her head toward the kitchen door. "What's up?"

"Good question," he said. "What a difference twenty-four hours makes."

"What do you mean?"

Mal shrugged, using the tines of his fork to gather up bits of crumb crust from his plate. "Yesterday we . . . Yesterday he came to find me at the bar. Did you know that?"

"No."

"He sought me out. He— I mean, he basically picked me up and dragged me home. And we talked for a long time. About all the stuff we hadn't talked about before. Yeah." He stared down at the plate, the fork, the remains of his pie; he couldn't eat it. "So we got back together. Or so I thought." He glanced toward the door Evan had just disappeared through. "I thought so . . . But now . . ."

"Now?"

"He hasn't met my eyes once all day," said Mal, setting his plate down. "The last time he wouldn't look me in the eye was right before he broke up with me."

Caro cocked her head. She was now leaning against the kitchen counter, her hair pulled back in a loose ponytail, her face a smooth pale oval with no makeup. "He's shy, you know. He always was, even before all the other stuff. Maybe it's just that?"

"We've been having sex for a while now, Caro," said Mal. "We kind of got past the initial shyness."

"But now it's more than sex."

"It is," agreed Mal. "It totally is. For both of us . . . That's why I think maybe he's going to dump me. Maybe this is what he does—he stays for a while and when it gets intense he goes. Comes back for a while, and then gets scared."

"Maybe he does." She fiddled with her bracelet, her eyes lowered. "Mal, I think— I think two things. One: if my brother needs to do that, then he needs someone completely trustworthy and faithful and patient, and I'm glad he found you, because no one could be more trustworthy than you."

"Thank you."

"But two: I also think that you deserve someone who isn't going to do that to you," she said. "You deserve someone who will stick around. So if you decide not to put up with it, I'll understand."

"Oh, that's not really in question. I'm in it for as long as he wants me. He knows that."

"Does he? You told him so?"

"I told him I was in love with him." Mal laughed. "No wonder he's outside in the cold, instead of in here."

She shook her head, gathering the plates and stacking them in the sink. "I swear, if he lets you go, he's more of a knucklehead than I realized."

"He is the way he is," said Mal. "And I love him. So who's the knucklehead?"

She was rinsing plates now, her brows knotted in a frown.

"Hey, you cooked." Mal nudged her away from the sink and took a plate from her hand. "Go sit down, start *Notorious*. Let me clean up."

"*Notorious*, huh?"

"Cary Grant plays a manipulative judgmental asshole."

"You're speaking my language," she said, and went into the living room.

Mal began to run water over the dishes. *It's okay*, he told himself. What he'd said to Caro was true. Evan was Evan; if he needed space, he would have space. If he needed sex, or affection, he would have that. Mal didn't know how to be in a relationship with someone like Evan, but he had his instructions from Evan's own mouth.

"Don't push."

It wasn't going to be easy. Maybe his love wasn't going to be enough.

Evan sat on Caroline's back porch, the November wind cutting through his T-shirt. He imagined himself slowly freezing, his blood thickening like gel with the cold, his bones turning brittle. Frost forming over his eyes.

Beside him, the kitchen window was open, and Evan, like a fucking asshole, had eavesdropped on an entire private conversation about himself.

I hate this. He rested his forehead on his knees.

He should be happy right now. He had reunited with Caroline, he had a really excellent boyfriend, and they were both being generous and kind, giving him food and affection and space. But he couldn't relax. He couldn't just exist.

Thanksgiving. His mind kept running and running, kept remembering—not Nez and the rapes, but before that. The En. Mom, thin and nodding and indifferent. Mom, screaming. Mom, suddenly silent.

He shivered. Fuck, he was so tired of not being okay. All day, pretending to be okay. And he thought he'd been doing it well too, laughing at Caroline's jokes, enjoying the movies. But they'd noticed. Mal, goddamn it, had noticed. Evan had hurt Mal, just by being his usual fucked-up self.

"I'm in it for as long as he wants me," Mal had said. But that wasn't fair, and wanting it to be didn't make it so. Right now Mal was probably thinking that being Evan's boyfriend was going to be a lot of fucking work. He was probably thinking of cutting Evan loose, before this got any more painful. Mal had already been let down, hard, by the people he loved the most. He'd be crazy to devote himself to someone like Evan. Maybe Evan had been right to break it off with him. For his sake.

No. *"Find a balance,"* that long-ago therapist had told him. *"Don't reject people because you're afraid they'll reject you."*

He hadn't been very good at taking that advice. His life wasn't balanced. But Mal . . . Mal did seem to actually love him. And Mal was smart. He knew what he wanted, what he could bear. He wouldn't appreciate it if Evan took that decision out of his hands.

Have courage, Evan, he told himself. And then, *Have a little courage, Alex.*

He shivered, got up, and went back inside.

Mal was alone in the kitchen, stacking dishes in the dishwasher. He glanced up at Evan, his dark eyes a little wary. "Hey."

"Hey."

Mal straightened, bracing his hands on the countertop, like he was waiting for a blow. But his voice was casual when he said, "Cold out?"

"Yes. I mean, no. I mean." Evan wrapped his arms around himself, still shivering. "I mean, *fuck* this shit," he snarled savagely, tightening his arms. "Fuck, Mal, some days I am so fucking sick of myself."

"Hey, whoa." Mal leaned close to Evan, not touching him, but surrounding him. "What happened?"

"Nothing happened," whispered Evan. He rested his forehead on Mal's shoulder. "Nothing has to happen for me to get this way. I just—I'm like a broken lamp or something. Sometimes everything is fine but I just don't feel right."

Mal whispered, "You're not a broken lamp. You're not broken at all. You're okay, Evan."

Evan's bones still felt like ice. "It's Thanksgiving," he explained weakly.

"Of course it is," said Mal calmly. "It'll always be a hard day for you, sweetheart. It's okay."

"I used to go to the ocean." Evan inhaled the smell of Mal's skin. "I wanted to be normal today, not weird-recluse-staring-at-the-ocean guy. But it's not working."

Mal turned his face a little, so he was pressing his cheek against Evan's head.

Evan pulled away and studied him.

Mal was so good-looking. *But it's more than that.* Mal had guts. He had the courage to reach out to someone like Evan, to be vulnerable to someone so imperfect, so untrustworthy. Evan would be an idiot to let him go.

Evan took a deep breath. "I need to leave."

"Okay."

"I'll say goodbye to Kiki, and then I'm going to head home."

Mal nodded mutely. His eyes were the dark clear brown of hot coffee, and there was pain there.

He thinks I'm breaking up with him again. I'm breaking his heart right now.

Evan shook his head. "I really think you would just let me do that."

"What?"

Evan grasped his shoulder and looked straight into Mal's eyes, so close to him that his vision blurred and Mal's face became a smear of color. "I don't wanna lose you," he said. "I know I'm a mess, but I don't wanna drive you off."

"You won't."

No? "If you still want to— Do you still want to come up to my place tonight?" Evan asked softly.

"I don't want you to do anything because you think you're supposed to." Mal's voice had dropped to a whisper. "Or pretend to be okay if you're not."

"No, I know. I know. But, Mal, do you want to?"

"Um, yeah. If you do. I brought an overnight bag."

"I do." Evan straightened, shaking tension out of his shoulders. "I'll go say goodbye to Caroline. Give me . . . Give me a little time. A couple hours. Hang out and watch movies. I'll see you later?"

"Okay. If you . . . Are you sure? We can do it another night if it's easier."

Evan tipped his head and kissed him: a warm, soft-mouthed kiss, like a promise. "Please come tonight," he said. "I want you to. Come sleep in my bed tonight. Is that okay?"

"*Yes.* Yes. If it's all right."

Evan nodded. "I'm sure, Mal. See you soon."

CHAPTER SEVENTEEN

It was nearly ten o'clock when Mal got out of his car in front of Evan's little A-frame cabin.

Dulcie was very nearly beside herself with joy. She leaped toward him like an impala, twirled like a ballerina, and then led the way to the porch with her head and tail high, emitting cries of glee all the while.

"I have never felt so welcome anywhere in my life," said Mal.

Standing in the doorway, Evan smirked. "Wait till I get you upstairs."

Okay.

To Mal's relief, Evan's eyes were alight, shoulders back, chin up. Quite a contrast to his appearance during Mal's first visit—the coiled, defensive posture, the hostile stare.

Tonight he seemed a little nervous, but Mal thought it was invited-my-new-boyfriend-over-for-the-first-time nervous, not about-to-freak-out nervous. "Are you feeling better, sweetheart?"

"Yeah," said Evan. "I took a walk. And did this mindfulness thing, like meditation. And a crossword puzzle. It almost always helps. Come on in. Keep your shoes on. There might be nails and things on the floor."

Coming in out of the dark, he could see that Evan's hair was damp, his skin flushed with a recent shave, and he smelled, faintly, of toothpaste. Mal imagined him showering, soaping up. Getting ready for him. He grinned and stepped into Evan's personal space, looming over him. "Thanks for inviting me," he said, and dropped a light kiss on Evan's minty lips.

"You're welcome," said Evan, politely.

Mal looked around the house: it was much the same, stripped-to-the-studs, sawhorses and toolboxes and bare wiring. All except for the kitchen, which was quite nice, with new cabinets and clean white countertops, blue and yellow tile backsplash. "What a *dump*," he announced. "Haven't you fixed this place up yet?"

"Not yet," said Evan, mild to his bitter. "Want a drink of water?"

"No, thank you."

"Food?"

"Nope, I'm full."

"Want to see the bedroom? I just finished it last weekend."

"Sure."

He followed Evan up a somewhat narrow and treacherous flight of stairs, and down a dark hallway, and then he was dropping his overnight bag in Evan's bedroom.

It was lovely. The space was a gabled nook under sloping eaves, with big windows. The cold rain pattering on the windows contrasted with the intimate coziness of the room: golden light, warm gray walls contrasting with crisp white trim, a worn oriental rug in soft blues and reds. In the center of the room was a big bed, covered with a puffy comforter, in a red and cream print. The room was like a little nest, lined with gray feathers, and smelled, very faintly, of new paint.

"Oh my God," said Mal. "You got the gay man's interior-decorating gene. Evan, this is gorgeous. Do you want to redo my town house?"

"Yes," said Evan immediately. "Your town house is so depressing."

A hand in the center of Mal's back and then he was falling forward onto the bed. He managed to flip over before Evan was on top of him, straddling him; Mal allowed him to pin his wrists to the mattress.

"My town house is quite tasteful," he said breathlessly.

"Beige," growled Evan, tipping his head so that his lips were millimeters from Mal's. "Beige walls, beige carpet, beige furniture. So much beige."

"Someday I'll introduce you to a shirt that isn't blue."

Evan laughed when they kissed, and *oh*, it was sweet. They kissed leisurely and long, Evan exploring him like he had all the time in the world. He leaned his weight on Mal's pinned hands, holding him still as he teased his mouth, kissed his jaw and throat, his ears, then returned to plunder his mouth again. Their legs tangled, groins and bellies pressed together. The length of Evan's cock was rigid against Mal's abdomen.

Fever swept over Mal's whole body, snatched his breath from his lungs. His own dick was stiff with excitement, his balls and nipples tingling. *Want to touch you.* He tried to lift his arms, but Evan wouldn't let him, kept him pinned and nipped his lip. Mal grunted at the sharpness of his teeth.

"Sorry," whispered Evan, and licked the spot apologetically, then tilted his head and devoured Mal's mouth. Mal made himself submit, let Evan control the pace and the intensity. Let him have whatever he wanted.

He ached for Evan. Not just to come, not just to get Evan off, but to be *with* him. He wanted to be joined to him, merged with him. He'd never felt like this before, so focused on one man, needing him so much. Not since Zach, but that had been a desperate, one-sided infatuation, not like this, not—

He moaned, inhaling Evan's kiss, unable to find any other way to express his desire. "Naked," he begged. "Please. Skin. Now."

"No," whispered Evan.

"You're driving me crazy," muttered Mal. Evan was still stretched out fully on top of him, pinning his hands, his thick cock aligned with Mal's through layers of clothing.

"I'm driving myself crazy," Evan admitted in a whisper. "Mal. I want . . ."

"Hm?"

Evan's face was flushed now. His lips looked bruised. His eyes were closed. "You love me," he breathed, grinding his groin into Mal's.

"Yes."

"I want you to fuck me," said Evan. "I want you to stop being so controlled and careful and just fuck my brains out. Tear off my clothes, throw me down, and fuck me. Like you don't care about anything, any of my— Just—just fucking fuck me, like nothing matters except fucking me."

Jesus Christ. Mal's dick voted *yes*. He heaved, flipped Evan off him, then rolled on top of him and stared down into his face. "Open your eyes."

Evan opened them. His pupils were huge with arousal.

At that moment, for the very first time in their relationship, Evan seemed passive. He gazed up at Mal, arms outstretched and hands open. He'd never shown this much vulnerability before. The sight sent lightning down Mal's spine, lighting up nerve endings from the nape of his neck to his balls. "That sounds interesting," he said, barely recognizing that throaty voice as his own. Evan's eyes widened a little. He didn't move, and Mal couldn't help but see the anxiety mixed with the desire.

Mal added, "You have to know I wouldn't do you like that, though."

"I'm not a virgin—"

"Uh-uh." Mal shook his head. Virgin, not-virgin, that didn't matter. He closed his eyes, reached for self-control, and kissed Evan, softly, just a brush of his lips over Evan's mouth. Evan arched up for more, but Mal eased away from him. "Call that Option A. Let's table Option A for now and revisit it at a later date. I have a counteroffer."

"You've gone all lawyery on me," murmured Evan.

Mal was now gently frotting him through their clothes. "I propose we instead select Option B: I fuck you sweet." He lowered his head and let his lips and breath graze Evan's ear. "I want to fuck you slow and sweet, and make fucking good for you, and we can spend all night fucking until we get it right."

Evan's breath was coming fast. He tugged Mal down for a kiss: wet and urgent and a little sloppy. Then he pulled back enough to say, "Option B puts a lot of pressure on you to please me, when—"

"So does Option A."

Evan shook his head a little. "No, in Option A you're so horny you don't care."

Mal thought he recognized Evan's mood—a sort of reckless capitulation, kamikaze submissiveness—*take me past this barrier, whether I like it or not.* But Mal definitely wasn't dom enough for that, and didn't think Evan was submissive. Not even a little bit.

He was betting on *bossy, demanding power bottom*, actually.

Mal leaned into him hard, pressed his body against Evan's, letting him feel his arousal, the quivering need in him. "I'm pretty horny," he agreed, roughly. "But I'm not *that* horny."

"Mal—"

"And then there's Option C, which is pretty much anything else. Blowjobs, Yahtzee, whatever. Tonight is B or C, sweetheart. Or B until you tell me you don't like it, in which case we revert to C. Your pick."

"I don't have Yahtzee," Evan whispered back, "so let's go with B."

I love you so much. Mal grinned. "Excellent." He rolled off the bed. "I'll get a towel; you take off all your clothes. Do you have lube?"

"I have lotion."

"I brought some lube. We're gonna need the good stuff."

He went into the master bathroom and let out a startled yelp—after the beautiful bedroom, the bathroom décor was a hideous surprise. Cracked lavender tiles, chipped salmon-pink facilities, ceiling a brilliant seafoam green that clashed sharply with tangerine walls. He grabbed a towel and escaped, laughing, back to the bedroom, where Evan was naked and lying on his side on the bed, pale and delicious, palming his thick red cock.

"Like the bathroom?"

"It's astonishing," said Mal sincerely, fishing a tube of lubricant and a box of condoms out of his bag and tossing them to Evan, along with the towel. He began to unbutton his shirt. "I gather it's typical of the original design aesthetic of this house?"

"They liked color, yeah," agreed Evan. "You're using a lot of big words."

"I'm kind of nervous."

Mal shucked out of his clothes. As he crawled onto the bed, Evan captured Mal's head in his hands and kissed him. "Why are you nervous?"

Naked together, there was no room for anything but honesty. "Because I fucking love you, and I don't want to make any mistakes."

Evan sighed and kissed him again.

They'd had a lot of sex, but this—bare together, deliberate and focused, with the lights on—this felt new and precious. Mal relaxed into the kiss and let his palms wander down Evan's smooth back—neck, shoulders, and back, that was what he had permission to touch. Evan snuggled closer though, trustingly, chest and belly and eager cock all warm against Mal. He was a little shorter and broader than Mal, and he fit perfectly into Mal's arms.

Mal was willing to do this for a while, kissing and stroking Evan's back, grinding their shafts together. But then Evan fondled Mal's nipples, sparking pleasure down his spine. "Oh my God, stop," Mal groaned, tightening his hands on Evan's shoulders.

"I could get off just like this," murmured Evan, then licked his throat.

"Fuck, I almost am." Mal was panting. "Stop. Later. Turn over, let me give you a backrub."

He sat on Evan's thighs and massaged his back until Evan relaxed, until he was purring and kneading the bed, spread out before Mal's eyes: The lovely V of his body, the wings of his shoulder blades, the columnar muscles on either side of his spine. And that pretty, perfect ass, oh yes. Mal was so hard now he was almost faint, his dick resting on Evan's butt where they could both feel it. But he had to please Evan. So he circled his thumbs on the dimples above Evan's tailbone, and said, "Let me touch you lower?"

Evan blew Mal's mind by spreading his legs and lifting his hips. He looked wanton and gorgeous, exposing himself. Voice muffled by his crossed arms, he said, "You could just push in."

Again Mal overruled the enthusiastic agreement of his dick. "That's not how I would prefer to do this. Let me touch you, Evan."

"Yeah. Okay."

Okay. Mal massaged the muscles of Evan's butt, enjoying the sight of his hands on Evan's pale cheeks, the way Evan was breathing harder. He poured some lube onto his fingers, and smoothed it down Evan's crack. "If you don't like something just say so," he murmured, fingertips circling slow and slick. Evan gulped for air when Mal found his snug hole. Oh, that was nice, that little gasp. "*No* is your safeword. *No, stop, ouch, what the fuck,* those are all your safewords."

"I don't think you understand what a safeword is," said Evan, spreading his legs so that Mal could massage his rim.

"I'm pretty vanilla," admitted Mal.

He took his time back there, just petting Evan, running his fingers over and around his pucker, his taint, his balls, watching his responses, listening. After a while he slowly slid a finger into Evan's body, and Evan's back arched like a stretching cat's. "Jesus, you are sexy," Mal said, entranced by the way Evan moved with the motion of his finger. "Do you ever do this yourself?"

"Ah—a little . . . sometimes—"

"This?" Mal curled his finger to stroke Evan's prostate, and Evan emitted a yawp. Mal bit his lip against a grin. "You like that?"

"Oh my fucking God."

More lube, a second finger. Slow. Evan keened with pleasure. "*Ah. God. No.*"

Mal pulled his fingers out, and Evan almost came off the bed. "Don't stop!"

"Shh," crooned Mal. "You said no."

"No, I meant, no, I never do that," panted Evan. "I didn't mean stop."

"Oh." Smiling, Mal penetrated him and found his gland again. "You like this?"

"That," groaned Evan, rocking his body. "*That.*"

"You really should."

"Yes, I fucking should."

Evan's gland felt swollen and needy, and Mal rubbed it rhythmically. He bent down, kissing the beads of sweat off Evan's back, relishing the salt, the way the smell of his arousal rose off his body. "I'll buy you a toy," he whispered, "and you can do this and think of me." He ran his mouth down Evan's spine, giving him plenty of time to protest, then crouched between his splayed thighs and used his tongue on Evan's rim, licking around his own probing fingers, tasting that sensitive, stretched flesh.

"*Mal,*" said Evan, sounding shocked.

Lasciviously Mal slid fingers and tongue over and into hot flesh. Evan was losing it perfectly, sweating, cursing, straining against him. "Mal, fuck me now. I want you to."

Shaking with desire, Mal found a condom, wrapped himself up, and poured on more lube. He lay on his side and pulled Evan back against his chest, cuddled him tight, little spoon to his big spoon. "Relax with me like this." Evan's head rested on his bicep, and their legs entwined. "Okay?"

"Uh-huh."

Mal rocked his hips, nudging his cock into the cleft of Evan's ass, and felt Evan shiver. "I like it like this," he said. "But I can't see your face, so you gotta talk to me. All right?"

"'Kay."

"Want to slow down?"

"I don't want to slow down."

"Then relax, sweetheart," he whispered.

He pressed in slowly, and it was so easy and so good, Evan's body welcoming him beautifully. They both gasped. Evan stretched out an arm and found Mal's hand, laced their fingers together. Mal's other hand grasped Evan's waist, fingers in the hollow of his hip bone, and he began to slide in and out of Evan's tightness, not deeply, gulping for breath and burying his sweating face in Evan's hair.

Oh, love.

Evan lay still, and he was being very quiet.

"Okay?"

"I—"

"Tell me." Mal kissed Evan's neck, his nape, his ear, stroked in and out. "Tell me if it's okay."

"Yes," Evan whispered. He shuddered. It was as if, in one moment, he surrendered all his doubts. He clutched Mal's hands and writhed, his hips rotating, fucking himself on Mal's dick. "Yes, yes, yes."

They rocked together, easy and sweet, but deeper now, and this was why Mal loved this position—their intertwined bodies side-by-side, this silken glide, the scent and taste of Evan's skin.

Had Mal said he could do this all night? What a hopeless boast. Not with the way Evan had caught fire in his arms. One hand gripping Mal's, the other clenched in the bedding, Evan's lithe body undulated. He moaned as he pressed his face into the mattress, meeting every one of Mal's thrusts.

Mal bit his lip hard. "Evan."

Without a word Evan pulled his own leg up, hooked an arm around his thigh to pin it against his chest, arching his back in a wordless, aching request for more. *So fucking hot.* "Evan," Mal said again. "Talk to me."

"Yes," panted Evan. "Yes. Oh God, Mal, I need it. You know what I need. Come on."

Mal gripped his hips and let his own pelvis snap forward in a series of quick, short thrusts, pulling Evan's body rhythmically back onto his dick. *Slow*, he told himself, but Evan was writhing, grunting. "Yeah, oh, Mal, faster. Faster. Mal. Fucking fuck me *faster*."

Bossy, demanding power bottom. Grinning, Mal rolled them over, put Evan on his hands and knees, rose above him, and then proceeded to give him the fucking he'd asked for.

"Oh, oh God," cried Evan. He was facedown on the bed, entirely vulnerable, with his ass up and legs spread. Mal was on top of him, inside him, overwhelming him.

Oh God, it was *great*.

He'd thought he'd be afraid in this situation. That this would make him feel helpless and used. But it was *Mal*. The hands that slid up his spine and pressed his chest and belly flush against the mattress, those were Mal's hands. That was Mal, taking him. Mal loved him, and that made him feel safe.

He trusted Mal, and that set him free.

Mal knelt between Evan's spread knees, hands braced on either side of his shoulders, thrusting into him with a rolling grind of his hips that drove Evan's cock and balls against the smooth sheets. "Oh my God," groaned Evan again. Then Mal shifted his angle and a bolt of white-hot fire shot through him, and he nearly screamed. There wasn't room in his thoughts for unwelcome memories, because— "Oh, *Mal*, oh fuck." Mal was nailing Evan's prostate with every driving thrust, dead-center. Again and again and again.

"Yeah?" demanded Mal. His voice was a growl. "You like it?"

"Yes," panted Evan. "Yes."

Mal's movements were controlled and commanding, a hard steady slam right to the center of Evan's pleasure. And Evan was *gone*, raising his pelvis with every stroke of Mal's, grinding on the mattress and fucking back onto Mal's dick. So good. So good. Oh, the feel of him, the feel of Mal taking him. Evan arched up, reaching. His nerves were lighting up like sparklers, he was gripping the headboard so hard his knuckles were white, pumping for all he was worth to get more, more, more of him.

Mal was clearly coming undone too. His sweat was dripping onto Evan's back, and he was beginning to groan on each exhale, those needy little vulnerable *ah*s he made when he was close, and the thought of his orgasm was enough to push Evan over the edge.

He spread his legs wider. "Mal, yes, I'm going to come— Mal! You're making me—" His spine stiffened, the muscles of his ass clenched hard on Mal's shaft, and the intense upsurge of ecstasy nearly stopped his heart. He pressed his face into the bed and shouted hoarsely, his seed streaming out of him, delight arcing through him like electricity. Mal was gripping his hips hard enough to bruise, gasping, hips jerking. Were the spasms that racked him his own orgasm or Mal's? He couldn't tell where he ended and Mal started.

They lay still, gulping for breath, for what felt like a long golden moment. His heartbeat gradually slowed, steadied, driving his blood through his body in long pulses that he could feel to his fingertips. *Bliss.*

He drifted in a daze for a while, uncaring that he was half-lying in a ridiculously large, cooling wet spot. Then Mal pulled out, suddenly clumsy, making Evan gasp a little. He heard the tiny squeak of latex as Mal tied off the condom, the damp *plop* as it dropped to the floor. With a sigh, Mal collapsed on his back beside him.

Anxiety washed over Evan like a cold bath.

What if he had a panic attack right now? How humiliating that would be, here, naked in bed with his lover. His *second* postcoital panic attack with Mal.

The thought was enough to shorten the breath in his lungs. He rolled onto his side, away from Mal, into the wet spot. He closed his eyes, and began breathing deeply, pulling air into his abdomen, imagining cool, clean oxygen pouring into his bloodstream.

Nothing is happening right now.

"Hey," said Mal, cuddling up behind him. "All right?"

Evan gave a little hum.

Mal didn't touch him with his hands, but he nudged and nuzzled. "Nope," he said lazily. "'Mm-hmm' is not going to cut it, I need words."

Evan continued to lie still, trying to slow his heartbeat, counting his breaths.

Mal tended to zonk after orgasm, lapse into a sweet endorphin haze, but just now Evan could feel him shake it off, go still and curious. "Evan." His voice was careful.

Give me another second. But Evan couldn't quite say it.

One of Mal's strong hands combed through Evan's hair, fingertips gently raking his scalp. He murmured, "You told me yourself that Option B puts pressure on me. So now you have to talk. Are you okay?"

Oh, nice, Evan was ruining this even *without* the panic attack. He squeezed his eyes shut. He was fine. Wasn't he fine? Yes, he was fine.

He just needed to be brave.

He rolled over, clasped Mal's face in his hands, and kissed him. Kissed him with all the gratitude and joy and fear and love that was inside him, because he didn't have the words yet. He kissed Mal until Mal whined softly.

Evan whispered, "I, uh, think I missed like sixty percent of the towel."

Mal's brows were drawn as if he wanted to ask questions, but he only said, "Okay."

Evan found the towel, and they wiped each other, mopping up sweat and come and lube and spit. His body felt loose, sloppy and well-used in his now-squalid sheets, and he realized he was smiling. He pulled Mal into his arms, tucked his face against Mal's throat. Mal tugged the sheet up over them, cool against their heated skin.

"I'm okay," Evan said. "Sorry. I didn't mean to zone out there. I'm good. I loved it. I loved it."

Mal's sigh brushed over Evan's skin. "That's good," he whispered.

"And I felt very safe. I wasn't scared," Evan said. "But then I sort of— Then I got scared that I was going to get scared. Which tells you how illogical and dumb I can be."

"Not dumb." Mal's voice had gone soft again, velvety. "Not scared?"

"No. Not at all. I loved it." Evan was starting to feel sleepy; it was comfortable, sharing a pillow with Mal, his arm slung over Mal's lean waist. "It was—it was really fast, wasn't it? Sorry."

"Amazing sex superhero requires no apology."

Evan pulled back far enough to squint at him.

Mal grinned. "I loved it too," he said. "That was great. We're still new at this and we're already killing it."

"Yeah?"

"I mean, the first time is usually all elbows and ears. We're world-class."

"Well, lucky for me you're apparently some kind of superhero."

"And you are absolutely incredibly gorgeous."

Evan ducked his head, drew himself into Mal's body again.

Mal sometimes did that—startled him with a compliment—and he never knew what to say. *No, I'm not* seemed argumentative; *So are you* was silly. So he just skated his fingertips down Mal's back. Mal shivered.

Evan did have something to tell Mal. Something too important to sleep on. "I eavesdropped on you and Caroline earlier."

"When?"

"In the kitchen, earlier today. I didn't mean to, at first, but then I did."

Mal was still. "Uh, what were we talking about?"

"You said you thought I was going to run away and come back. Come and go, like a visitor in your life. Too scared to stay for long. Like a user."

"Oh, *that* conversation." Mal propped himself up on an elbow, looked down at Evan. "I don't think I put it like that."

Evan couldn't quite meet those intelligent brown eyes. "You weren't wrong," he said, one hand smoothing over Mal's arm and shoulder. "I haven't been able to stay away from you since I met you, but I haven't been able to stick around, either. And I'm— I do sometimes just need space, need to be alone. I might have to get away from you sometimes, for a few days. Or a week. Not because you did anything wrong though. And I don't know how that works when you're somebody's boyfriend." He forced his eyes up to Mal's, knowing that his face was an open book. "But I want to keep coming back to you, Mal. If you'll let me."

Mal caught Evan's hand in his own, laced their fingers together. "Yes," he said, simply.

"I won't be with anyone else," Evan promised.

"I won't either. I don't want anyone else."

"Caroline said she thought you deserved better."

"No—"

"She wasn't wrong either." Evan cupped Mal's face in his free hand, touched his forehead to Mal's. "But I'll always come back to you. If you want me to. Trust me?"

"I trust you."

"I've never trusted anyone this much in my life. I don't want you to get tired of me—"

"There is zero chance I'm going to get tired of you," said Mal. "You take as much time and space as you need. I'm like a rock. I'm not going anywhere."

"You are like a rock." Evan kissed him. "You know I love you, right? I love you so much."

Mal's breath hitched slightly. "I love you too."

"Love you so much," murmured Evan, nestling into Mal's arms.

And then, like a man exhausted after putting down a heavy load, he fell asleep.

CHAPTER EIGHTEEN

"**O**f course I don't mind a bit," said Mal's mother. "Since you were busy. A whole group of us went to a lovely restaurant across the river in Vancouver. The Grant House, do you know it?"

"I don't," said Mal.

As he did every year, he had joined his mother for day-after-Thanksgiving dinner in the dining room of Cedar Heights Assisted Living in Troutdale: tired turkey covered with gravy, even tireder Brussels sprouts, cranberries, yams. The stuffing was pretty good, if you liked stuffing.

"Well, it was quite nice. They served duck confit and salmon as alternatives to turkey, which I think is a very good idea. Some people think Thanksgiving isn't the same without turkey, but really, it's not the most flavorful meat." She was currently cutting hers into perfect squares. "It's nice that they offered some options. Don't you agree?"

"Absolutely."

"So as usual I didn't miss you at all."

He smiled at her. As often happened, he was struck by how young she looked. She was dressed in a tulip-pink skirt suit with a flower-shaped brooch on one lapel, and her hair had been freshly touched-up and styled to wave softly around her face. She had been forty when she'd had him, her only child: right now she looked no more than fifty. "I'm glad," he said. "As usual, I had dinner with my friend Caro." He braced himself. This was one of the unexploded mines of their relationship: why he and Caro had always spent Thanksgiving together, instead of with their loving families.

"And how is Caro?"

"She's doing well. And her brother joined us, this time."

"Oh?" asked Dorothy, coolly. "*Caro* brought family to your Thanksgiving?"

Ouch. "Well, it's an unusual situation. I'm dating her brother. So in a sense, I brought him as my date."

Bright and clear as the diamonds sparkling on her fingers, her eyes tracked the slight redness of beard-burn around his jaw. She might just have seen the edge of a hickey on his neck, peeping up from the collar of his shirt. "Oh. Really," she said. "I wasn't aware that you were seeing anyone."

"It's pretty new."

"But you took him to Thanksgiving. So it must be serious."

Mal put down his fork and knife carefully.

Goddamn it. After all these years, did he still have to explain himself to—defend himself from—his mother? Hadn't they already *done* this?

He said, with as much ringing clarity as he could manage, "It is very serious. I am in love with him, and I am going to put a ring on him." *If I can get him to stand still long enough.* "And it doesn't matter to me if you like it or not."

She sipped her water. "It shouldn't, Malcolm," she said. "I just think you might have introduced him to me. Since it's apparently so serious."

He got a grip on his temper. "You know him, actually. He works here at Cedar Heights. You encouraged me to ask him out. It's Evan Doyle."

That did surprise her. "You're engaged to Evan Doyle?" she demanded, in a voice loud enough to attract the attention of the others in the room. People all around them turned to stare. A low hum of talk began to fill the room. What a juicy piece of news this must be. Gossip spread outward in an almost-visible wave.

He slapped a hand to his forehead, squeezing his eyes shut. "Not— We're not—"

The man at the next table gave a little snort through his white moustache. "You are or you aren't, young man," he said. "Don't be wishy-washy."

"Why don't you mind your own business?" Mal suggested, through a sharp-toothed smile.

"I agree with Mr. Willison, Malcolm," said Dorothy, nodding approvingly at the moustached man.

The room was buzzing with words like *ring* and *lawyer* and *in love with Evan Doyle*. This was a catastrophe. Evan *worked* here. Mal said desperately, "I just haven't asked him yet, because it's still new. I'd appreciate it if you didn't mention it to him."

"You're keeping it a secret?" asked Dorothy, again just a little too loudly. Someone at a table behind him gasped.

Mr. Willison said gruffly, "Disrespectful. That boy hasn't got any family, you know. If you're going to do it, do it properly, out in the open."

"Thanks for the tip," said Mal. "Mom, it's not a secret. I just haven't—"

"Well, you should get on it," she said. "Mr. Willison is quite right. Nobody likes a man who isn't decisive."

The old man puffed his chest, and Mal restrained himself from rolling his eyes. He leaned forward so that his words wouldn't be heard by anyone but his mother, and hissed, "Exactly when did you become such a Pride-flag waving gay marriage supporter?"

She regarded him. For a moment, her face reflected her true age. "Your father loved me."

Taken aback by the non sequitur, he said, "I know. I remember."

"Andrew loved me too." Around them, the other residents were returning to their meals and conversations. "But they both died, and no one else liked me much. Andrew's children were adults, and they had no interest in a relationship with me. You were gone." He didn't respond, and she said, "I know, Malcolm. That was my own fault. All of it was. It seemed so clear, once I was alone, that I hadn't been very likeable. So I decided to try to do better."

Mal picked up his cutlery and resumed eating his turkey. They ate in mutual discomfort.

All his life, she'd never known how to express emotion. Obviously she still didn't. He hadn't, either, until he'd left home and found a band of people who hugged and said "I love you" the way his mother's people had said "Good morning." And then he'd found Caro, who was even more cautious with her heart than Mal, and who had needed family just as badly.

One of his cuff links clinked against the rim of his plate. He was wearing the blue enamel ones she'd given him. They did look good with his navy suit. He touched one, thoughtfully.

No, Dorothy wasn't good with emotions. But she always remembered birthdays. She gave great gifts. Thoughtfully selected to be perfect for each individual, beautifully wrapped, accompanied by a gracious personalized card. He'd always found her gifts annoying, as much a display of class and wealth as an act of generosity. But that wasn't really fair. Dorothy devoted time and effort to those gifts. They were a sign that she was trying.

She couldn't say the words, his mother. But she *was* trying.

The least he could do was try to meet her halfway. "Mom, I'm glad you moved out here. I'm glad that we got to know each other again."

"I'm glad too," she replied immediately.

"And I could use a little help. Would you do a favor for me?"

She brightened. "Of course I will. What is it?"

"When I— I mean, if I ask him, in the future," he said, cautiously, "I'd like to have rings picked out. Wedding rings, not engagement. You have great taste, and you know him. You could pick out a ring that he'd like. Can you do some shopping and come up with ideas?"

"I'd love to. Nothing too ornate for Evan. Nothing with stones. But not a little narrow circlet, either. He could wear a wide band."

"Send me your ideas," he said. "Seriously, though, don't tell him. And even if I do ask him, he might not say yes, so don't actually buy anything. But if . . ."

"It's good to be prepared." She nodded. "Maybe with two or three options. It shows that you're a conscientious man. I'll look into it."

"Thanks, Mom." She looked like a general with a plan of attack, and battle in the morning, her eyes alight with determination. Or maybe like she'd been waiting for years for him to ask a favor. He smiled at her. "That would be great."

After dinner Mal went back to his town house alone and turned on a movie, which he didn't watch. Instead, he sipped beer and remembered last night, every detail.

Evan loved him.

Evan might not know how to be in a relationship. Mal might not know how to be in a relationship with a man with chronic anxiety. He might push too hard. Evan might draw away. They might get their wires crossed, might miscommunicate, might fall apart. Maybe it would be hard.

But it wouldn't be boring. And Evan loved him. Evan loved him.

God, it was such a simple thing—millions of people achieved love every day. But somehow it had been out of Mal's reach his whole life. For a long time his heart had felt a little twisted and hard, like a juniper that had seeded on a cliff. Its growth had been stunted early, from his father's severity, the inconsistent and conditional nature of his mother's approval. Then blighted by the shocking loss of Zach. He'd limped along from relationship to relationship since then, trying this and that, never really trusting, never fully healing. He'd had sex, plenty of it, but no one who loved him, nothing that made him feel whole.

Well, Caro loved him. She was like a sister, and finding her had undoubtedly saved him, but a sister's love couldn't fill the ache of loneliness that had settled into his bones, night after night.

But now, Evan. His love felt like a balm, soothing and loosening some tight knot of caution inside him. He trusted Evan with his heart, and by some miracle, Evan trusted him too.

He wanted to dance with joy, wanted to run outside and do a solitary *Singin' in the Rain* number right in the street.

Instead he just hugged himself, sipped his beer, and laughed.

Sometime in the night, the mattress shifted beneath him, and he woke from a deep sleep to find Evan sitting on the side of his bed.

"Hey." Mal rubbed his eyes. "What time is it?"

"After one." Evan's expression wasn't visible in the darkness, but the dim light from the window showed that he was dressed in underwear and a T-shirt. "I used your key. I used your shower. Is that okay?"

"Yeah. Of course."

Evan hesitated, and Mal was suddenly worried that something was wrong. Evan had never come there before uninvited, except when Mal had been sick. Mal wanted to wrap his arms around Evan and pull him into bed. Instead, he kept his arms at his sides. "Did you get some dinner?"

"Yes."

"Everything all right?"

Evan nodded.

"Then come to bed, sweetheart."

Evan crawled under the sheets and stretched out beside him, not touching. "Just to sleep, okay?"

"Sure."

Mal turned his pillow over, cool side up, nestled down under the blankets, closing his eyes. Listening to Evan breathe in the darkness. He could smell Evan's wet hair.

After several minutes, Evan said, "So, I went by work today to pick up my jacket that I'd left there."

"Oh, shit." Mal sat up. "What did she say?"

"She? The whole place was talking about us. About seven people congratulated me on our upcoming wedding. Gloria Anderson told me she knows of some very tasteful venues."

"Oh God." Mal flopped back down onto the pillows, squeezing his eyes shut. "Oh man. I am so sorry."

"You told your mom you wanted to marry me?"

"I told her we were dating. It kind of took off around the room. It was scary."

Evan turned on his side toward him. "So you don't?"

Mal gathered his courage. "No, I do. But I know it's too soon. I know I need to not push you. My mom will push, though."

"Oh, I know."

He looked over at Evan, wishing he could see his expression. "We haven't figured out how any of this works yet. We haven't even figured out how to sleep together yet. I don't want to pressure you into anything."

"But is that where you see this going?"

"I would be open to that. If you think so. But yeah. Yes, I do."

After a moment, Evan said, "Okay. Good night, Mal."

Mal smiled wryly. "Night, Evan."

They lay together for a long while, wrapped in darkness, a few inches of space between them. Mal wished Evan would come a little closer, relax with him, but he didn't move. *Don't push.*

Just as he was relaxing toward sleep again, he felt Evan shift, roll toward him. They quietly negotiated the space, awkward and unused to touching without sex, until they found a way to fit together: Mal's head resting in the hollow between Evan's shoulder and chest. Evan's heartbeat was slow and steady under his ear.

Then Evan pressed his feet against Mal's leg. They were like ice cubes, cold enough to make Mal gasp. Mal loved that he warmed his feet on him though, loved the way they fit. He imagined a future, when they were a little more familiar with each other, when he could complain about Evan's cold feet.

After a while he said, "Want to eat an apple out of my hand?"

"Shut the fuck up." Evan shoved him away.

Mal laughed.

Evan grabbed the pillow and pummeled him, and Mal rolled into a giggling defensive ball. They wrestled a little, and then Evan pulled Mal into a hug and spooned him.

"My jackass boyfriend," muttered Evan, tucking Mal tight against him, twining their legs together.

Mal smiled in the darkness. "My woodland creature."

Dear Reader,

Thank you for reading Jenya Keefe's *Relationship Material*!

We know your time is precious and you have many, many entertainment options, so it means a lot that you've chosen to spend your time reading. We really hope you enjoyed it.

We'd be honored if you'd consider posting a review—good or bad—on sites like **Amazon, Barnes & Noble, Kobo, Goodreads, Twitter, Facebook, Tumblr,** and your blog or website. We'd also be honored if you told your friends and family about this book. Word of mouth is a book's lifeblood!

For more information on upcoming releases, author interviews, blog tours, contests, giveaways, and more, please sign up for our weekly, spam-free newsletter and visit us around the web:

> **Newsletter**: riptidepublishing.com/newsletter
> **Twitter**: twitter.com/RiptideBooks
> **Facebook**: facebook.com/RiptidePublishing
> **Goodreads**: tinyurl.com/RiptideOnGoodreads
> **Tumblr**: riptidepublishing.tumblr.com

Thank you so much for Reading the Rainbow!

RiptidePublishing.com

ACKNOWLEDGMENTS

Thanks are owed to lots of people, but mostly to Mary and Glenn.

ALSO BY
JENYA KEEFE

Ángel and the Elf-Lord (coming soon)

ABOUT
THE AUTHOR

Jenya Keefe was born in the South. She has an advanced degree in European history, and has spent much of her life working the kinds of jobs a history degree qualifies you for: gift shop employee, lumber grader, classifieds clerk, hot glass artist. She currently lives in the Seattle area, where she works at a library. She has always written stories.

Website: jenyakeefe.com

Twitter: @JenyaKeefe

Tumblr: tumblr.com/blog/jenyakeefe

Enjoy more stories like *Relationship Material* at RiptidePublishing.com!

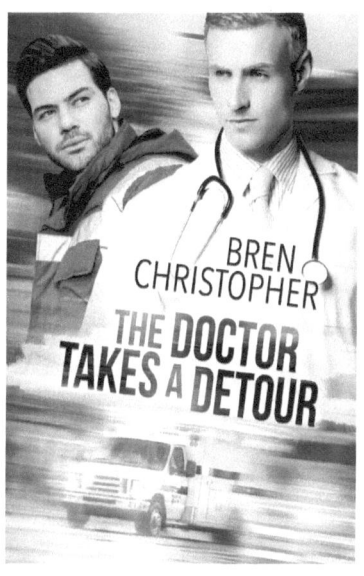